EMPTY DEVILS

CHRIS DILEO

SOBELO BOOKS

Book cover by Matt Seff Barnes
Edited by L.C. Marino and L.P. Hernandez

Formatted and published by Sobelo Books

ISBN (paperback): 978-1-965389-11-9
ISBN (hardcover): 978-1-965389-13-3
ISBN (ebook): 978-1-965389-10-2

First edition, 2025

Praise for Empty Devils

"*Empty Devils* is a surprisingly complex and beautiful treatise on grief, hate, memory, and monsters. DiLeo writes some kick-ass bloody action then follows it up with gut-punch passages about love. The ending will haunt me for a long time." – **Sam Rebelein**, Bram Stoker Award-nominated author of *The Poorly Made and Other Things*

"Aggressive. Heartfelt. This book is going to piss all the right people off. What would you do if a monster took away your child? Where would your anger lead you? The perfect story for today told by one of horror's most dynamic voices." – **L.P. Hernandez**, Nazi Hunter and author of *No Gods, Only Chaos* and *In the Valley of the Headless Men*

"A bloody tale of loss and vengeance, *Empty Devils* is razor sharp and cuts deep. The "fuck your feelings" crowd will hate it." – **Chris Panatier**, author of *The Redemption of Morgan Bright*

ALSO BY CHRIS DILEO

Hudson House

Calamity

Blood Mountain

Meat Camp (with Scott Nicholson)

The Devil Virus

Dead End

Dark Heart

Revival Road

Children of Fire

The Hands of Onan

What Ever Happened to Jo Rose?

What Darkness Waits

Contents

DEDICATION

For Jenn, whose love and belief carries me through.

"What's done can't be undone."
William Shakespeare

Part One

"Grief fills the room up of my absent child,
Lies in his bed, walks up and down with me,
Puts on his pretty looks, repeats his words,
Remembers me of all his gracious parts,
Stuffs out his vacant garments with his form;
Then have I reason to be fond of grief."
William Shakespeare

Chapter One

With my daughter in a casket and my wife in a cult, I went to see the skinheads.

The August morning was hot and humid, the air thick and slimy.

The wannabe Nazis infested a two-story shotgun house on a backroad fifteen minutes from my home. Paint peeled from warped boards, shingles dangled loose, and six motorcycles crowded the dirt yard. Harleys and Triumphs. High-end, well polished. One alone cost more than the house. A truck was parked on what little grass there was. Easier to drive over the lawn than mow it.

A big-chested white guy in a wife-beater leaned back in a rocking chair on the porch, slurping Bud and sucking the spillage off his ratty mustache. His head was shaved bald. His feet in heavy boots were up on the railing where hung a Make American White Again sign.

The air stank of sweat.

"Morning," I said from the street.

The guy leaned farther back in the chair. It creaked.

A Confederate flag dangled from the side of the porch roof, and an American flag from the opposite end. A blue medical mask sagged from a nail in a porch post.

"I'm David Eden." I pronounced it loudly and clearly.

He swigged the beer and sucked his mustache. "You a Jehovah?"

"A Jehovah?" I chuckled. "That would be surprising."

The can didn't make it to his lips this time. "You some weirdo?"

"Absolutely. It's hot as hell and I'm in a damn suit. At least I remembered my sunglasses."

"You *are* a Jehovah."

I pretended to think about that. "I'm a teacher."

Another slurp. "School sucks. Teachers thought they were so smart."

"You must hate smart people."

"What?"

"They must make you feel so dumb."

"Oh, man," the guy said, "you *are* crazy."

The grin I offered did nothing to dispel his conclusion.

I got into teaching twenty years ago because I loved stories and language, but I stayed—and might well stay another twenty, assuming this week didn't kill me—because I loved the kids. From the over-achieving, high-stressed APers to the bound-to-drop-out-of-community-college, please-give-me-a-65ers, I loved interacting with my students, hardheaded and apathetic alike, and I was good at sizing up a kid quickly, knowing how to handle and best motivate even the most challenging cases.

I was nobody's Teacher of the Year (too many students liked me for my colleagues to be anything but skeptical), but Mr. Porch-Rocking Beer-drinking White Supremacist could've been one of my seniors in English 12 a few years back, and I would've won him over him with good ol' boy talk about engines and girls, and I might've gotten him to give a damn about something more than prejudiced thoughts and beer, perhaps even care about a character in a story or a line in a poem. Except he wasn't a former student, and I wasn't here to talk poetry.

But I was here to teach a lesson.

"Let me ask you something," I said. "You like my suit?"

The man stared as dumb-eyed as a cow, pulled his legs and dropped forward. Miracle the chair didn't shatter. Or the porch. He shook a finger at me. "I know exactly who you are."

"Too bad. I was hoping we could play Twenty Questions."

He stood. When he wasn't drinking he was lifting weights, and on the small porch he had a significant muscular presence. "Yeah, I do," he said. "You're an asshole."

I stepped onto the yard. Dirt puffed around my dress shoes. It'd been a few weeks since a good, drenching rain. "Indeed I am, but I'm also David Eden. My daughter was Penelope Eden."

My voice broke on her name.

Recognition, or something close to it, dawned on the man's face. "You should leave."

"No doubt," I said.

Another few steps and I stood over a Harley. It had a large black seat, bags attached on either side of the back wheel, and a metal holster holding a shotgun.

"This can't be legal. Not in New York."

"Fucking nanny state."

"State law," I said, "and probably town, too. Warrenville Town Board doesn't want Main Street turning into Mad Max country."

Looked like he almost understood the reference. "You a detective or something?"

A detective? That was an idea I sort of liked, but I shook my head. "Let's go with 'or something.' " I touched the shotgun stock. "You don't read the papers, do you?"

"Papers?" The man rolled his shoulders, puffed out that big chest, but did not step any closer.

Without looking down, I asked if there was a lock on the holster.

"You gonna pull it on me, that it?"

My fingers played on the stock. "Is it loaded?"

"Who are you?"

"David Eden. Who are you?"

The man had to think. "Jessie," saying it with defiance.

"Where's your buddies, Jessie? Jerking each other off?"

Jessie's face crimped into rage that resembled an infant the moment before crying. "You got some balls."

"Are you asking to jerk me off?"

Jessie was so stunned he couldn't say anything, his face scrunching even more and getting redder.

"Don't be embarrassed. We're living in enlightened times. Embrace who you are."

He stomped one booted foot, a bull about to charge.

I raised my hands, palms open. "I'm here to talk."

The heavy foot came down again.

Sunlight glinted off a chrome muffler, and somewhere in the woods that cocooned this house, a dog barked three times.

Jessie paused with his foot ready to come down once more. He grinned and his boot settled to the porch without a sound. "You gonna wish you wore running shoes." Jessie's teeth crowded his face.

My collar was wet, my mouth dry, and my chest tight. It felt like my ribs were squeezing my heart. My fingers tingled pins and needles. I massaged them, one hand and then the other. Slow. Methodical.

"The phrase," I said, "is not 'you gonna.' It's 'you're going to.' You are going to wish you wore running shoes. It's intentional, though, right? Colloquial phrasing to further distinguish you from me, to draw the proverbial line in the lexical sand." He looked completely confused. "Oh, come on, Jessie. You're dumb, no doubt, but you can't be *that* dumb."

Jessie stopped at the porch edge, leaned forward. "Fuck you."

He spit a fat glob on the dirt.

"What else could we discuss? American history? The race problem?"

He smirked. "The poor Black people. *Wahn. Wahn.* They were freed like three hundred years ago. How long it take to get your shit together?"

"Your math needs as much work as your grammar."

"Fuck off."

"Well said. Now, is there someone of authority with whom I can speak? Anyone in the house who isn't preoccupied with onanistic self-gratification?"

Someone moved in the doorway, looming in shadow behind the screen door. Maybe two or three someones.

"Hello?"

"I'll stomp your face in," Jessie said.

"Clinging to cliches. And what was the transition into your threat? You can do better."

Jessie's smile faltered and he chugged the rest of his beer, throat flexing, dribbles trickling down his neck. To complete the stereotype, he crushed the empty can, dropped it, and kicked it off the porch.

"And now you're littering." I made a *tsk-tsk* sound.

A door squealed open on the second-floor porch, and a shirtless man emerged. Tall and muscular, though not to the meat-head level of Jessie, this guy was clean-shaven, had a crew-cut, and was covered in tattoos. Among the designs on his chest and sleeving his arms: the numbers 14 and 88, the letters HSN, and, of course, a Swastika, so large it stretched from his chest halfway up his neck. Something like that was easy to remember.

"You're Erik," I said.

The man betrayed no surprise. He was in the background of a photo that got national distribution, not to mention all those retweets from both sides (#WhiteEvil, #StoptheHate, #BLM, #Antifa, #SaveAmerica #FreeSpeech), so he expected to be recognized. *Hoped* to be, no doubt.

"You lost? Car break down?"

"Thought I'd take one of these bikes."

"You ride?"

Another trio of barks. Closer.

"Can't be much to it," I said.

"Which one you want?"

"The one with the shotgun."

"Good choice. Have to ask Leroy."

"Leroy? Haven't had the pleasure."

Jessie grunted, probably thinking it a gay reference.

"He's inside. Doesn't like being woken up."

"Must've been tough to get him up Saturday," I said. "Protest started at ten."

"You might be right." Erik looked around—the woods, the trailer park beyond—nonchalant, just another day in White Paradise.

"What about you, Jessie?" I asked. "Were you there? Were you one of the degenerates chanting censorship and hate?"

"Fuck yeah, I—"

"Five words, Jessie," Erik said.

Jessie closed his mouth, stepped back from the porch edge, a reprimanded child, and said, "I have nothing to say." Reciting it like a good little boy.

I caressed the Harley's leather seat, the gleaming handlebars. A beautiful machine, not that I knew anything about motorcycles.

"You here to cause trouble, you might as well get on with it."

"Okay. I'll start by kicking this dimwit's ass."

Jessie was shaking his head. "*Man,* you gonna pay."

"*Going to.* We just went over that. Remember?"

That brought Jessie forward again, not stopping this time, coming down the steps, boots thump-thumping.

One hand on the handlebars, I reached behind me with the other, slipping beneath the flap of suit coat.

Erik was saying Jessie's name again, calmly, bored with this responsibility, but Jessie was waffle-denting the dirt, biceps and shoulders tensing, hands balled into heavy fists. He might outweigh me by sixty pounds. Maybe eighty.

"Jessie," Erik saying it in a sing-song way he might call a dog. "Spill blood on this property, Joe'll be pissed."

Jessie hesitated a half-step but decided, in what limited capacity he possessed, to damn the consequences.

In this regard, at least, we were on the same page.

Jessie was cocking back an arm for a full-swing haymaker, but with the Harley between us he would have to fully extend himself, come off his feet a bit (he was big, but those heavy arms could only reach so far), and that gave me the advantage.

As if he knew what the hell I was doing.

My hand found the leg of the wool sock dangling from my back pocket.

"Jessie . . ." Erik was saying again.

"*No,*" Jessie said, "this shithead's got it comin'."

He stopped before the bike, face scrunched and crying-infant red, and he swung as I ducked, yanking the sock from my pocket, and then I hurled it into Jessie's armpit.

The billiard ball nestled inside the sock *thwonked* hard and Jessie exhaled a crackling cough, toppled sideways, falling, hands slipping away from the bike.

Inertia stumbled me into the Harley and my homemade weapon swung back to dent the fuel tank.

Jessie groaned, stared up at me and said through his teeth: "I'm going to kill you."

"Look at that," I said. " 'Going to.' You're learning."

Someone joined Erik on the upper porch (it was not worthy of being called a balcony)—a woman barely past her teenage years, so skinny and pale she might be a captive, stashed in a closet and fed scraps. She draped onto Erik, her body all angles and knobby protrusions.

"What the hell . . ." She sounded drugged.

She could be pretty if she got some sun, ate some food, shampooed the grease from her hair, and stopped smoking weed or snorting coke or whatever it was she did. The way she looked, the girl would be as dead as Penelope in a few months, half-year at most.

"Who's that guy?" She pointed.

The mortician would rouge her cheeks, darken the skin a bit, wouldn't want a corpse appearing too corpse-like. But she wouldn't require any special reconstructive work, wouldn't be beyond repair, wouldn't be so mangled the funeral director could only shake his head.

"What's he doing?"

"Shut up, Mercedes."

Maybe Penelope had known her. Everyone lives a secret life. Children included. My daughter had all her drawings, which were a secret life of sorts. And my wife, well, she had a secret life of an entirely different sort.

I raised a hand to wave and was yanked forward into the bike.

Jessie had the ball-end of the sock in one hand. He pulled. I tried to grip more tightly, but the wool slipped through my fingers and missed the re-grab, and I ended up stretched over the bike, staring down at one pissed-off idiot.

Spit slipped off Jessie's lips. He pulled himself onto all-fours—billiard sock bumping over the ground—and stood.

"Jessie—" Erik said again.

"You play dirty, old man," Jessie said. "I'll teach *you* something."

I straightened, hands on the bike.

Jessie made a *huck-huck* noise that might've been him trying to chuckle but sounded like he was choking. He raised his arm. The weighted sock hung like a medieval flail, minus the spikes, thankfully.

Not that it mattered. I hadn't come here expecting anything other than a conflict. Maybe I'd leave limping or on a stretcher, or maybe they'd drop me in a hole in the backyard and piss on my grave. Didn't matter, at least that's what I wanted to believe, because I wasn't going down without a fight. My daughter deserved that much.

If I shoved the bike—

Three sharp dog barks. Directly behind me.

Jessie lowered his arm and grinned.

"I walk the dog," a man said, "and look what I come back to."

I turned and flinched.

The man was tall, strong, and handsome, wore black boots with red laces, black jeans, a white tank-top that showed off a scatter of tattoos, but he had short dark hair, gelled, and his expression suggested intelligence or at least a level of discernment above the likes of bottom feeders like Jessie.

The dog was a beautiful Siberian Husky, white and grey with blue eyes and it was ready to play, stretching to the end of its short leash, tail wagging, tongue lolling.

Any dog kept by these assholes would be a product of beatings, verbal assaults, and starvation. One word from the man holding the leash and this dog would tear out my throat. Except the dog didn't look cowed, or dangerous, or even hungry. Thirsty maybe, but otherwise healthy and playful.

"Cerberus," the man said, "sit."

The Husky backed up a step and sat. His tail swept the street.

"Gorgeous dog."

"Thank you." The man took in the scene—Jessie and Erik and Mercedes—without concern. "It was a beautiful morning for a walk, but I take it that's not why you're here, Mr. Eden."

"Ah, shit," Erik said.

"What? Who the fuck *is* this guy?"

"Shut up, Mercedes."

"Hey, fuck you, Erik."

"Jessie," Erik said, "did you know who this guy was before you went Ivan Drago on him?"

Jessie spit, wiped his mouth.

"Who is he? Who's Ivan Drago?"

"I told you to shut up." Erik made as if to hit her and she swept out of range and fell awkwardly against a railing that would've snapped had she weighed even ten pounds more.

"This is David Eden," the man with the Husky said. "Father of Penelope Eden, who so recently shuffled off this mortal coil."

"Fuck's that mean?" she asked. "Who the fuck *is he?*"

The man, whose name was Joseph Klegg, started to respond but I cut him off: "It means my nineteen-year-old daughter was murdered by an asshole white supremacist driving a 1977 Dodge Charger, Midnight Edition. He was going seventy-plus miles-an-hour when he hit my daughter. Both of her legs shattered and her lower spine snapped on impact. She was tossed into the air, crashed onto the windshield, breaking her right arm and fracturing her skull, rolled up onto the roof and fell off the side onto the street, fracturing her skull again and her sternum and also breaking six ribs, one of which pierced her myocardium. That's the tissue around the heart. So, my daughter, who was a sophomore art major at SUNY New Paltz, who was holding a Love is Life sign made from cardboard and written in Sharpie with pink hearts on it, died in the middle of Main Street not twenty minutes from here when her rib punctured her heart after she was hit by a car driven by someone *you* considered a friend. That, Mercedes, is what the *fuck* that means, and who the *fuck* I am."

No one spoke.

The day had gotten much warmer and sweat soaked my undershirt. My heart was hammering, trapped and frantic, my every muscle tensed. I had no weapon. I was not in anything resembling top physical shape, but I had my pain and my grief, and they were my armor and my weapons. They electrified my nerves, crystalized my vision, and signed the warrant of my own destruction.

So be it.

"You could kill me right now," I said. "Use my homemade weapon to do it. Drop me in the woods and say you never saw me. Poor bastard was probably so struck with grief he beat himself to death. People'll believe it. It's got a narrative roundness to it."

Jessie raised the sock. The billiard ball made it rock side-to-side and I thought of the grandfather clock in my mother's house. When I was a little boy, I would sit cross-legged in front of it and count the seconds as the pendulum swung. I once did it for two hours straight and walked through the rest of the day in a fog.

I clucked my tongue to the sock's swaying rhythm.

"He's crazy," Jessie said.

"Of course he is," Joe Klegg said. "His daughter died four days ago and he's wearing this suit because today's her funeral." Joe stepped closer. The dog watched, tongue dribbling. "You were there," he said to me. "You watched it happen. Why weren't you at her side? I bet she asked you to protest with her, hold up a sign. Stop the Hate. Love is Freedom. Imagine if you'd agreed. When that car barreled toward her, you could've pushed her out of the way. She'd be alive and you wouldn't be here in an ugly suit trying to get yourself killed."

Something lodged in my throat, my eyes burned, and my fingers throbbed. If I made any movement, I'd be launching myself at this man in blind madness, punching and thrashing and screaming. God, how I wanted to.

"That what you want? Me to kill you? Send you to your daughter?"

I heard the screams, the engine roar, the *thunk-thunk-thunk* of body against bumper, roof, and road. *She's dead. Your daughter's dead and you watched it happen.*

"My daughter," I said slowly, not moving my jaw, "did not shuffle off this mortal coil. She was *murdered.*"

"Lemme do it, Joe," Jessie said.

I clucked my tongue again—steady, time-keeping.

Joe's boots crunched into the dirt and the leash pulled the dog beside him. Cerberus should've been growling, but he was all jolly panting and tail-wagging.

"You want me to kick your ass? Think that'll bring Penelope back?"

"Don't. Say. Her. Name."

"Other people were hurt. Including my associate, Rando. He's in bad shape. Might not make it."

"My daughter was not hurt." My voice wobbled. I hammered it flat. "She was brutally killed."

"And the alleged perpetrator, Tanner Wyatt, is in jail," Joe said. "I expect if he ever makes bail, he's the one you want to have this conversation with."

"You put him up to it," I said.

"If that were true, he wouldn't have come from the east, which put some good brothers of mine in harm's way. I would've had him drive down a side road, Freedom Way maybe, then cut over, a more direct route to the protestors. Is that what you want to hear? Because the truth is that Tanner's an unstable guy, always has been. He watched that Charlottesville video over and over, thought that driver was a hero."

"What if he's wearing a wire?" Jessie said, worried.

The man's stare did not leave mine. He had grey-blue eyes like his dog. His face was almost movie-star handsome. "There are stages to a man's grief," Joe said.

"Huh?" Jessie grunted.

"Five stages," saying it like a professor, "denial, anger, bargaining, depression, and finally, acceptance. Anyone want to guess what stage Mr. Eden is in?"

"You tell me, Joe, what stage is confront the Nazi assholes who murdered your daughter?"

"I was there, too, Mr. Eden. Wyatt could've run me over."

"Which idiot flag were you waving, Confederate? Nazi? Aryan Brotherhood?"

"I don't wave flags." He grinned. "But if you want to discuss philosophy and ethos, please come inside. We might be able to broaden your perspective."

Like Erik, Joe had the expected tattoos (the numbers, a skull, a cross, and a Swastika, though smaller and almost tactfully nestled under his collarbone), but when he gestured to the house as if welcoming a guest, I saw the black spiderweb tattoo on his elbow. That was special. Meant he'd killed someone for the brotherhood.

"You're an educated man, Mr. Eden. Master's in Literature with a concentration in Shakespeare. You teach the college-bound at the high school. You think you know me, but I do know you. Always good to know who might be coming. So, please, let's talk. I'll make coffee."

Spit in his face. Strangle him. Smash his skull against the road.

"You got it all wrong. There aren't five stages of grief. I'm not here to bargain or forgive. Grief has one stage—anger."

Joe nodded, snapped his fingers as if remembering something. "We can't talk. You have a funeral to attend. Which church is it? I'd like to pay my respects."

"Fuck you, you worthless piece of shit."

"So much pain," Joe said, calm as a therapist. "You need to let go."

"I need to exterminate all of you."

Joe's lips spread wider. "This conversation is over." He leaned closer. He smelled of aftershave. "I'm going to say this once: Don't come back here. You get a pass this time. You're a grieving father. There won't be a second pass. Come back and this ends very differently."

"That's bullshit," Jessie said. "He hit me. I'm going to burn his house down and—"

"Shut up."

Jessie did.

"You make that homey sock yourself?"

"Yes. I even wrapped the ball in tape so it wouldn't split."

"Cue ball?"

"*Eight* ball."

Joe looked amused, even pleased. "Give it back to him."

Jessie held it out. I had to turn from Joe to take the homey sock and part of me expected Joe to sucker-punch me but he didn't.

Jessie mouthed an ugly epithet and I took the sock and swung it at his face. He dodged it, falling back, lost his balance, fell into another bike, and man and machine sprawled together. Cerberus barked three times.

Mercedes hiccuped laughter.

"Oops," I said.

"Funny," Joe said. "That's good. You must feel pretty proud of yourself. I want you to remember that when you get to the church, when you walk between the pews toward the altar, when you sit down and listen to the priest eulogize about life everlasting, when you realize why you're there, when you stare at that coffin, when you remember what's in it, when you understand that once you were a father but not anymore."

Swing the sock. One good hit to the skull. End this now.

"My sincerest condolences, Mr. Eden."

"We are not done," I said.

But it was getting late. My daughter was waiting.

Chapter Two

They couldn't start without me.

The people in the pews watched me walk down the aisle. Someone coughed. Someone else snorted into a tissue. My eyes burned. Had I been crying? Was that before or after I tried to play action hero with a bunch of numbskull white supremacists?

What about your grand plan for vengeance? What happened to teaching those ignorant assholes a lesson?

My father and Julie's parents sat in the second pew on the right. My father leaned forward, his trembling hand pressing a handkerchief to his face.

Across from them, young people looked dazed and uncomfortable. Penelope's friend Case, short for Cassidy, sat at an angle so her leg jutted out, its pink cast covered in Sharpied hearts and messages of love. She'd been next to Penelope when it happened.

Case got a cast and Penelope got a coffin.

Case and the other girls in the pew were wearing pink shirts with my daughter's face on them, smiling big inside a heart.

The coffin was bright white and cost several thousand dollars. I might have bought one ten times as expensive if the mortician suggested it.

White roses heaped on top of it.

The priest, a skinny man with a sunburned face, stood behind it. He nodded at me. Was I supposed to nod back? I had an incredible urge to give him the finger.

The front pew waited—empty.

I sat and the priest spoke and my daughter's funeral began. People stood and sang, kneeled and prayed, sat and wept. I mourned tearlessly. Memories fought to be considered. Anger promised release. My hands wouldn't stop flexing until I tangled them together and squeezed. Pain felt good. So I squeezed harder.

The priest stood at a tall lectern, something right out of an old Puritan Church, and read Scripture. The story of Lazarus. The man Jesus resurrected.

In the story, Jesus says he is the resurrection and the life and whoever believes in him, though he die, yet shall he live, and whoever lives and believes in him shall never die, and Lazarus's sister Martha agrees—her brother will live again at the final resurrection when God returns. But Jesus (and I'm slipping a bit here into imagination) shakes his head and says it's good your brother died because now I will prove I am the son of God, sent here to save the world. He asks to be brought to Lazarus's tomb where, as everyone knows, he commands Lazarus to "Come forth" and the dead man emerges from his tomb after being interred four days. That was all well and good for Martha, and presumably for Lazarus (though strangely he never speaks and no one asks him about his experience or even how he feels, he's simply loosed of his grave clothes and left to go where he will), but what about all the other brothers and sisters and sons and daughters? Why does Lazarus get a second chance at life and everyone else gets, at best, a promise of eventual resurrection in the Final Days or at worst, a lame bullshit metaphor?

"The Gospel of the Lord," the priest said.

"Praise to you, Lord Christ," the congregation responded.

Except for me. I was clucking my tongue, keeping time.

The priest gave his homily, but I didn't listen. I stared at the coffin and felt the space around me expand larger and larger. The empty pew might be as large as the church itself. Dad cupped my shoulder. His weeping was a strangled, sloppy mess. I was alone, and I *wanted* to be alone. I would not play the part of wounded son for my father. I moved out from under his hand.

Silence stretched and stretched, a caesura of dry coughs and fabric rustlings and cellophane crumblings, and I would let the moment keep stretching, infinitely, all the way to my deathbed; because so long as I stayed right here in this empty pew with my daughter in a box, I would never have to stand above as that casket descended into the ground, never have to toss one of those white roses on top, never have to hear all the condolences and apologies and promises to keep in touch, never have to thank people for coming or for baking me lasagna, never have to explain why Julie wasn't—

"Son?"

The priest was staring down at me. His red face was absurd. The white sphericals around his eyes made him look somehow insectile. Had he been sunning himself poolside when someone called to say David Eden's nineteen-year-old daughter was run-down on Main Street, and if so did he simply turn over to get an even tan?

"Son?"

Not the priest speaking—Dad.

I stood, knees popping, and the priest gestured toward the coffin like a game show host revealing the grand prize.

Congratulations, you win a dead daughter in a box!

This was so completely absurd. I should've laughed.

Instead, I gave in and played my role: the grieving father who approached the coffin on slow but steady steps and placed a hand on it at full arm's length and dropped his head. It would make a striking photograph, especially with the light filtering in through the stain glass windows.

"She was my Ellie." My voice did not crack, did not even betray the tremor in my heart. People would say I was in shock or that I was handling this well, bearing up with incredible strength. "She was my Little Ladybug, my Little Monster, my Penny Candy. She was my daughter."

People stared. Waiting. Someone honked into a tissue. So odd everyone in their funeral clothes. Dressed up for someone who couldn't see them.

Among them, my friend Corbet and his wife. His jaw was firm.

I opened my mouth, had no more words, and closed it again.

The priest took up words instead and the empty spot in the front pew waited. My father and Julie's parents watching, red-eyed and beaten. Penelope had loved her grandparents, and they'd adored her. And there she was between them, maybe six years old in a pink-and-purple Easter dress, swinging her legs, white buckle shoes not touching the floor. It was so vivid. The pink barrettes in her hair. Her hands flattening her dress against her legs over and over until Grandma Irene placed her hand on Penelope's. *Be still, dear.*

Little Penelope watched me return to the pew. Staring at me, curious. Her eyes brightened. She smiled a big grin that showed off the gap between her front teeth that braces would eventually fix.

"Son?" my dad said.

I blinked. Little Penelope was gone.

"Son?"

I didn't respond. I didn't sit. I walked down the aisle and back out into the burning summer sunshine.

Chapter Three

I went home where my daughter was waiting for me.

After the protests in Charlottesville in the summer of 2017 that killed a 32-year-old woman named Heather Heyer—crushed beneath a Dodge Challenger driven by a white supremacist—my only child took to wearing a shirt with Heather's face on it.

"What's with the shirt?" I asked. She was fifteen then, eighty percent of her life already over. A few years later, her friends would sit in church wearing shirts with her face on them. Was that irony? Or cruelty?

"Solidarity," Penelope said. She was standing before the open fridge, its cold light glowing around her, a slice of provolone curling over her fingers.

"My Penny Candy," I said with exaggerated awe. "The great avenger of injustice."

"I hate that name, Dad."

"I know you do." She waited, knowing what was coming. "Penny Candy."

She rolled her eyes in the overly dramatic way she perfected before she was ten.

"I also see you're trying to refrigerate the entire kitchen."

She sighed, extra-extra dramatic, and opened the fridge door wide as it could go. She curtsied from the door and then swung her arms up in a carnival barker gesture. "Behold," she said, "the magic fridge of the Eden household. Never before has a fridge been so powerful, so astounding in its capacity of frigidness, so utterly and completely and arctically *cold*. Come see this magical wonder before the electric bill is too high and the fridge must be forever turned off!"

Her smile was so beautiful. Though I'd read about such things long before Penelope was born, I knew firsthand the truth: There is no love like the love you have for your child. They can break your heart a hundred times a day and mend it back just as easily and as often.

"You really think you're funny, don't you?" I said.

"I take after you, Daddy-O."

She smelled the cheese on her finger and darted her tongue out for a quick, cat-like taste. It was cute, had been when she started doing that as a little girl and still was now as a teenager. All that bullshit my mom used to say about me always being her baby no matter how old I got turned out not to be bullshit at all. When pulmonary failure wheezed out her last breath, I was holding her hand just as I once had when crossing the street was only safe with Mommy at your side. Children were supposed to bury their parents. Not the other way around.

"You know I'm forty, right? I was a teenager in the nineties. We didn't say 'Daddy-O.' "

"Should I call you 'home skillet' instead?" She folded the provolone into her mouth.

"I never used that slang, either."

She said something but it was a garbled mess around the cheese, so she settled for sticking her tongue out. Eight years old again and asking me if I knew what her favorite food was and I asked what and she said, "See food." and opened wide.

"You've matured so much," I said with that same exaggerated awe.

She swallowed. "With a father like you, how else could I turn out?"

"Well played . . . And yet the fridge remains open."

The eye-roll again, but she finally closed the fridge and hoisted herself with ease onto the counter, pink-socked feet tapping against each other. "There's a rally in Newburgh today."

"For what?"

She made a *what-do-you-think?* gesture and pulled the end of her shirt out to showcase the face on it and the words printed there: "We're standing up to hate."

"That's the slogan? Why not 'rise above the hate' or 'love over hate' or 'crush the hate,' 'smother the hate,' 'demolish the—' "

"Daaad." She said in that tone which could rapidly get more impatient and ever more sarcastic.

"Too negative, huh? 'Scorch the hate'? Well, you don't fight fire with fire, so what about 'extinguish the hate'?"

She gestured for me to continue. "Get it all out."

I shook my head. "Wouldn't want to ruin the suspense."

Three times (four times?) the charm for the eye-roll, and something struck inside me I couldn't articulate, but which took me right back to my mother's sallow face, red-rimmed eyes, her papery skin, my hand holding hers, and the dying words she couldn't enunciate: *My baby.*

"Uh-oh," Ellie said. "The old man's having a moment. Is it a stroke?"

"And you think *I'm* funny."

"All *relative* in this family," she said.

"I thought we had a strict no-pun policy in the house."

"No, Dad." She leveled her gaze. "You mean a 'no-*fun*' policy."

Hands to my heart, I stumbled backward. "Ouch. Score one for . . . Penny Candy."

Ellie hopped off the counter and crossed the kitchen toward me. She had her mother's face, her father's wit (or lack thereof), and a young woman's youthfulness, but as she neared she was the teenage girl in baggy GAP hoodies who could be so sweet and so bitchy and who drank pickle juice like it was Gatorade because she thought it would give her bigger breasts (way to go, internet); and then she was the high school graduate who spent hours decorating her mortarboard with glitter and marker she then refused to toss into the air at commencement; and then the little girl with long, curly red hair who stared up at me as if my six-foot height qualified as gianthood; and there she was as that eleven-year-old who giggled at everything; and then the fourteen-year-old who had a crush on a boy named Bobby Day, same name as an oldies singer famous for "Rockin' Robin," which Ellie used to dance to when she was only two and which I sang every time the crush was mentioned; and there she was at five, crying at her reflection in the bathroom mirror and clawing at the freckles on her nose another kid said looked like dirt; and the crying was so similar, despairing and phlegmy, when she called from college late one night after the first boy she'd truly fallen in love with (and who thankfully did not share a name with anyone famous) had broken up with her; and here she was, my daughter, my only child, standing right in front of me, and my eyes were leaking, though not crying, as if I knew what waited in her future and in mine.

"Jeez, old man, maybe you *are* having a stroke."

She let me hug her before sighing, giving me one more really good eye-roll, and strolling out of the kitchen into the dining room where a shaft of summer sunlight streaming through the windows glowed around her like it does around angels in religious paintings. Something tweaked in my chest. All these heartbreaks, no way I could ever be whole.

"What're you doing, Dad?"

The light was gone, and Penelope was staring at me. Nineteen years old, beautiful, and wearing the same shirt she died in. On it, a Gandhi quote inside a big pink heart: *Where there is love there is life.*

Who says God doesn't have a sense of humor?

"What're you doing, Dad?"

"Nothing."

Talking to my daughter's ghost?

She tilted her head in that questioning way that was as judg-mental as it was inquisitive.

Alas, poor ghost! Speak. I am bound to hear.

"You're quoting Shakespeare in your head, aren't you?"

"That predictable?"

"You always have this face when you're thinking of the *Bard.*"

"A look of deep literary contemplation?"

Even her ghost could eye-roll. "Constipation."

I feigned offense, brought my palms to my mouth, and blew my lips against them in a terrifically loud wet fart noise.

Back when she was Pavlov-responding to Bobby Day's song by spinning in circles, she also collapsed in giggling seizures anytime I made a farting noise, the wetter the better.

"Dad, seriously," Penelope's ghost said. "You shouldn't be here."

I should be avenging your murder, most foul.

She sighed. Funny, a ghost could be impatient.

"No, Dad. I want you to—"

"Don't say it—"

"Return to my funeral."

"I know!" Screaming at ghosts, oh, how Shakespearean. "Never shake thy gory locks at me, child," I said, quoting Mac-beth to Banquo's ghost. I'd said it once to Penelope when she came home after using a friend's pool and she shook her wet hair at me like a dog, splattering a chlorine stink everywhere and making a ghost's *Booo!* sound.

"You should be at my funeral."

"So should your mother."

"Dad . . ."

"She gets a pass but I don't?"

Penelope didn't respond because, yes, Mom got a pass and I didn't. That's what mental illness does for you.

Penelope and I sometimes called it *the crazies*, as in, *Mom's got the crazies again.*

Better to say that than say, *Mom's searching for all the knives you hid* or *Mom's been scrubbing Clorox into the bathroom floor for hours and hours* or *Mom's standing naked in the yard talking to the birds* or *Mom went to that occultist in Beacon again and now she's high on some herbal potion.*

"She's not in a hospital," I said. "Not at some mental health clinic. She's at a women's cult."

Ellie didn't dignify this with a response.

You realize she's not really there, right? She's in your head. You're talking to yourself. Worse: you're talking to an empty house.

"I had a plan."

I did, too. It wasn't much, but I wasn't completely unprepared. I had the homey sock I'd carefully made, wrapping electrical tape around the eight ball again and again, and the old ash tree in the backyard could testify to my practice swings, bark fragments littering the ground and the trunk nicked and dented, its raw flesh exposed in places I'd pretended were people's faces.

"Your plan was to beat them up?"

"My plan . . . was to kill them."

"With a billiard ball in a sock?"

I wanted to tell her that was the best I could do and that should mean something because at least it was *something*, I wasn't moping around in a puddle of grief or absconding off to some feel-good cult—I was confronting the people who took my daughter from me. Who *killed* my daughter.

"Why today when it's my funeral?"

Come on, we're going into town, we used to say when we were adolescents on bikes back in the nineties, and if one of us said *Nah,* we'd shrug and say, *Your funeral.*

My generation was one of the last to grow up with freedom enough to spend all day away from home without having to check in. Parents did whatever they did and we went about being kids. Now, with phones in every kid's pocket, parents were perpetually scared of an unanswered ring, an unresponded to text, terrified their kid might vanish into darkness.

I knew better. Stay in touch all you want. Your kid can disappear right in front of you. Your kid can die right in front of you.

"Go back to the church, Dad. You'll regret not being there."

"Why?"

"To say goodbye."

"You're right here."

"I'm not."

I could feel her there, her presence. If I touched her, would I feel the softness of her skin, the pumping blood in her veins, or would my hand pass through her?

Worse—would she be cold and stiff, dead?

"I'll go. For the burial. I'll meet them at the cemetery."

That Penelope-look again, the judging stare, the tilted head.

"What?"

"You're lying."

I stuck out my tongue.

"You need to grieve."

"Ah, to weep is to make less the depth of grief."

"Stop with the Shakespeare shit. I'm dead and—"

"No, you've merely shuffled off this mortal coil."

"Dad, enough. You're hurting and you need to accept this."

"But to die, to sleep, to sleep and perchance to dream, ay, there's the rub—"

"Dad, stop!"

In the quiet, the fridge compressor hummed.

Now that the dead are yelling at you, maybe you're *the one with the crazies.*

"Please," Penelope said. "Go back to the church. It's not too late."

"It *is* too late."

I reached to touch her . . .

Sunlight sliced across my hand.

And she was gone.

The kitchen was empty. The house was empty. A mausoleum now.

I had that walking-in-a-fog sensation again, same as I had after counting the seconds tick-ticking on that grandfather clock. I clucked my tongue. My ribs cramped tighter. I couldn't breathe. The house felt huge yet also shut up tight around me. Sealed shut like a coffin.

How could absence be so stifling?

Everyone can master a grief but he that has it. Shakespeare again.

Chapter Four

I couldn't stand there forever. Maybe Penelope had gone up to her room. Vanished to her room? Ghosted? I headed that way but I never even made it to the stairs. What was the point, sit on her bed and sob? Weep at her cork board of motivational quotes and pictures, at her art award ribbons, flip through her sketchbooks as if to find a secret message just for me—*Sorry, Daddy-O, I love you*? It was all so goddamn cruel. Why not stand right here and sob? No matter where I went in the house, it would be the place where Penelope had lived, the dining room where she twirled a goofy pirouette in that ladybug dress and knocked over Mom's Tiffany's vase, a million fragments scattering so far and wide we were finding shards for weeks after, or the living room where Penelope chomp-chomped popcorn at me on the couch as we watched *Jaws*, kernels falling all over, or the downstairs bathroom where she puked for what seemed like days when she was only five, the stomach flu turning her blue-lipped and so sallow-skinned we brought her to the emergency room, holding her on my lap in the waiting room, wiping the sweat from her brow and rubbing her back, but that was also the bathroom where she spent an entire day getting her glittery prom dress to fit just right and redoing her makeup three times before she was ready for pictures. Why go up to her room at all? My daughter lived everywhere. Forget my bedroom where she spent so many nights sleeping between Julie and me, sprawled so I balanced on the bed edge, because the boogeymonster was going to get her, or that same room where she burst in with her phone raised high, startling me out of a nap, the screen bright with her email from SUNY New Paltz: Congratulations and Welcome!

She'd gone to college but now I'd been accepted into my own institute of higher learning. *Congratulations and Welcome to the College of Grief and Suffering! Here you'll study emotional pain and loss over and over again and you can also suffer extra hard and earn an advanced degree!*

No. There was nowhere to go where Penelope wouldn't be.

I was still dressed for her funeral. I should go back to the church or at least head out to the cemetery. At least do *that* much.

My ribs were crowding in tightly. Pressure was building within me. I would not stand here and scream or cry or just wait.

"If I go to your funeral, will you speak to me again?" I said it loud, an announcement. No response, not from her, anyway. A little voice spoke up in the back of my head, *Already at the bargaining stage. We're moving right along, aren't we?*

"Fuck you."

I went out into the backyard where the sunlight was so strong it blanched all colors.

The old ash tree was enormous. Its trunk at least five feet wide with massive branches thick as trunks themselves tentacling out, reaching higher than the roof. It was a gorgeous tree, and Penelope had climbed plenty high and often enough to tempt fate and yet she never fell, never once broke even a single bone. Some branches were now completely bare. Dead. Old or diseased, yet I bet a car could barrel right into it and it wouldn't even budge. Cruel irony, yet again.

A souped-up engine was revving. Down this street or a block over. A teen with his sports car, maybe, or a middle-aged man with his mid-life crisis.

Louder and louder, a growling whine and there was Penelope staring up into the sun during the protest, everyone around her chanting "Love over hate! Free Speech! Free Love!" and my mouth was greasy-slick from two slices of pizza, my heartburn coming on, and I heard the engine, its scream louder and louder, and I looked away from the pink-and-purple-clad protestors and from Penelope, her face tilted into the light, a smile on her lips, and there was the enormous Dodge Charger, bulky old and *fast fast fast* and in the scattering screams my daughter had no time to move and it hit her and the sunlight gathered around her, lifted her, and dropped her back down. Then we were all screaming.

I was squinting into the sun. My eyes burned runny tears. My jaw throbbed. Could you clench so tightly you broke your own teeth?

I needed to hit something.

I went to the tree.

I'd done some good damage: the dented, fractured bark, the wood pock-marked from my swings, yet the fleshiness that had been so pulpy raw was now darkened, healing. Well, I could fix that, couldn't I? The homey sock, however, was in the car. *Punch it,* I told myself. Instead, I cursed at it, spit at it, and turned back to the house.

Penelope was at the small patio table, sketching in her one of her pads. It wasn't on the table; she was curled in the chair so her butt pressed up against her feet on the cushion, the sketchbook was on her thighs, and she was shading with fury, like she was mad at what she'd created.

Who needs ghosts when memories are everywhere?

She was ten or eleven and focusing so intently she didn't notice me creeping up on her to spy the sketchpad. She began drawing, as in *really* drawing, only a year or so earlier but her skill was impressive, human eyes so detailed they might be photographs, landscapes with watery reflections and subtle shadows so startling I thought she must be tracing something.

I remember the moment when her drawings were not simply something a young child did, crayon-scrawled stick-figures, but might be for her an actual talent, a calling. A sketch of her bed, detailed down to the dangling flap of wrinkled sheet and beneath the bed a pair of menacing eyes above a gaping fang-toothed mouth. A horror-movie moment, my mind already suggesting there was a demon in her room or it was possessing her and when I asked her about it she would say, *It won't let me sleep.* Except, that isn't what she said.

"That's the boogeymonster?"

"It won't bother me anymore."

"Because it's not real?"

She looked up at me. "Of course, it's real."

I had no response, but whatever it was never again startled her screaming awake in the middle of the night to send her burrowing into bed with us.

Since then, she'd drawn vampires and werewolves and all sorts of hybrid creatures a mad scientist might create, awful things with claws and fangs and fur and fins and tails. Alien creatures with bulbous heads and spider legs. Sketchbooks full of them. She never became the weirdo sleepless kid in horror movies. She was always upbeat, empathetic, beautiful. She just liked monsters.

"Another one?" I was behind her on the patio.

She paused mid-shading. "A little one."

"Can't you draw pretty things?" It came out sounding more serious than intended.

"But vut do you mean, Zaddy?" She put down the sketchbook and turned toward me, her upper lip tucked so her teeth looked huge, eyebrows arcing up her forehead, and she hooked her hands into claws, and she slowly stood and high-knee stepped toward me. "Zon't you zinc I vam pretty?"

"You're my little monster."

Another step and she attacked with a Dracula roar. I caught her in an embrace but before my fingers found her ticklish spots along her ribs, she was a high schooler hugging me just because, and all I could do was squeeze back and hope it could last forever.

"Can't you at least put one in a dress? That ladybug one you used to wear?"

"Dad, I was, like, four."

"You were cute, my Little Ladybug." She made a face, but it wasn't completely dismissive.

"I need one of your drawings. Draw me beating the shit out of those assholes. That's what I need. Draw it so I can believe in it."

But she wasn't there. Penny had finally broken a bone. Lots of them, in fact. And they would never heal. They'd remain broken, suspended by arteries plump with embalming fluid.

That revving engine turned my head like I had sudden dementia and had no idea where I was. Memory or reality? Didn't matter.

What mattered was that the people responsible should not get to carry on as if nothing happened. They killed her. Tanner Wyatt was behind the wheel, his booted foot on the gas pedal, but I blamed them all. From the idiot goon Jessie to the wannabe-capo Erik to the too-smart-for-his-own-good leader, Joe Klegg. Hell, screw Mercedes, too. Who gave a shit how she ended up with those idiots? She wanted to be counted with them, she could damn well suffer with them.

What mattered was getting justice.

That sports car engine revved louder. *Louder.* I turned back to the house and there was Penelope, her face filling the world, blue veins squirming in translucent skin, eyes black stone, and her mouth stretching too, too wide, white lips quivering around the engine-scream howling out of her.

Then she was gone.

CHAPTER FIVE

I went back to the skinheads.

Two guys were on motorcycles next to each other, taking turns firing the engines back and forth in a mechanical pissing contest. One was a heavy guy in a sweaty tee-shirt, he on the Harley with the shotgun holder, the weapon missing, and the other was good old Jessie, fully recovered from earlier and even changed into a clean undershirt. Still had that ugly mustache, though.

No one on either porch. No other motorcycles and the truck was gone, too.

I parked directly across the street.

Jessie and the heavy guy saw me get out of the car and approach but they kept at it with the engines. It vibrated inside my molars.

The homey sock dangled from my right hand. It tapped my leg as I walked.

I stopped several feet away and Jessie smiled his mouth of yellowing teeth as his motorcycle engine screamed.

Fifty-one tongue-clucking seconds passed before they cut the engines.

"Man," Jessie said, "you are crazy."

It took effort to unclench my jaw. "I know we were working on your grammar earlier, but we should also focus on developing your vocabulary. What are some synonyms for 'crazy'?"

"This the guy you talking about?" the heavy one said, sounding like he was speaking with his mouth full. His cheeks bunched his face the same way his gut wadded his body. He was easily three hundred pounds. "You dented my bike," he said. His bottom lip bulged.

"Not my fault. That was Jessie's fault. Right, Jessie?"

"You gonna try to hit me with that thing again?"

I sighed. "Back to 'gonna' I see, and we can do better than 'thing.' As I was just saying . . ."

Jessie got off the bike. "Joe said give you a pass, but he also said don't come back but here you are."

"Here I am."

"Joe ain't here and neither is Erik."

My mouth was dry, my grip on the sock tight as it could get.

"I'll give you one hit with that toy of yours," Jessie said. "After that, I'm going to kill you. Leroy gets to watch."

I nodded, considering. "Leroy, were you at the protest on Saturday when my daughter was murdered?"

He hocked a splat of brownish liquid into the dirt.

Jessie rolled his shoulders, twisted his neck into successive chiropractic pops. He cracked the knuckles on both hands. "Ready when you are."

I didn't move.

Gee, an inner voice mused, *what's wrong? I thought you wanted vengeance. I thought you wanted to kick this guy's ass and damn the consequences, even if it ends with you coughing out bloody shards of broken teeth.*

I took a breath. Leroy spat.

Gently, I started rocking the billiard ball at my side.

Clucking in time with it.

Something near worry but closer to confusion weakened Jessie's tough-guy expression, but only for a moment. "Go ahead. Swing, crazy man."

He thunked a boot forward and I stepped sideways. The next step flattened a clump of crabgrass and then we were in motion like two circling animals sizing each other up.

"I said we could do better than 'crazy.' How about demented? Insane? Lunatic? Deranged? Unhinged? You know any Latin, Jessie? *Non compos mentis*? What about Shakespeare? I've been on a real Bard kick lately. Maybe I've eaten on the insane root?" *Sure sounds like it,* I thought and laughed. "Or am I but mad north-north-west?"

Leroy sucked at his cheeks, readying another fat glob. He looked as bored as if he were really in a classroom.

"Shut up and come at me," Jessie said. "Or are you a pussy?"

"Oh, good, insult my manhood. Want to be Lady Macbeth and tell me to screw my courage to the sticking place?" I laughed. It sounded like a rusted hinge.

"What is this, your next stage of grief or whatever?"

"Nope. Still anger."

A door opened and someone said, "What the hell is this? He came *back?*"

This time appearing on the front porch, the girl who looked like a captive, Mercedes, was wearing a white summer dress with red polka dots on it. They almost looked like ladybugs. *My Little Ladybug,* I thought.

Leroy spat a thick clump, and I looked up and saw Jessie's fist a moment before it hit my face.

Down I went.

Jessie was laughing. His boots kicked up dirt.

"Leave him alone," Mercedes said, coming down the porch steps.

Jessie kicked at my foot, as if I might attack.

Then he leaned over, hands on his knees, but before he could say anything I sat up and swung the homey sock. It caught his nose, and I swear I heard the cartilage snap. He blurted a surprised scream, stumbled a few feet, cupped his nose, and said in a nasally voice: "Now, you're dead."

I smiled at how silly he sounded and the thick sole of his boot filled my vision and he broke *my* nose. I blacked out, I guess, because then Mercedes was kneeling over me, the sun flickering her into Penelope.

And back again.

Chapter Six

"Jesus, Dad. You're such an idiot."

Penelope tucked a curl of red hair behind her ear. Her eyes were shining like dew on morning grass. *Do ghosts cry?*

"You sound like Mom," I said. My voice off, woozy, like I was drunk.

Maybe I was.

"Somehow I doubt that." The voice was deep and masculine and Penelope was now my friend Corbet Willis. "You must be on some good drugs."

"What the hell happened?" I asked, even though I knew. Jessie, moron that he was, had taught me a lesson and now I was in the hospital, and the only wonder was that he and Leroy hadn't killed me or given me brain damage.

Well, you are interacting with the ghost of your child, so maybe brain damage isn't entirely out of the question.

"You tell me," Corbet said. "I found you passed out all bloody in your car."

Corbet taught chemistry at the same school where I taught English, and he loomed over me the way he did his students, muscular body, gleaming bald head, eyes wide, the whites a startling contrast to his black skin.

"My car?" I sounded congested, my breathing muffled. I investigated the bandages on my nose and unplugged the bloody swabs from my nostrils.

"In your driveway. So tell me: Did you break your nose and bruise four ribs falling down the stairs and then get in the passenger seat of your car because you were disoriented and then pass out?"

"Shit. The burial."

His hands caught my shoulders, eased me back onto the hospital bed. A machine beeped several times.

"It's over. We buried her."

Emotion without name smacked me like shovelfuls of dirt.

Like the way it must've smacked the coffin when they buried her.

I tried to push against him again but it didn't work. I cursed and punched the bed. Fading light hazed the window. Must be late.

"Why'd you walk out?"

"Yeah, Dad," Penelope said, appearing on my other side. "Why'd you walk out? Afraid you'd seen a ghost?"

Real funny, honey. I clamped down on those words. No point in Corbet thinking I'd lost my mind.

"Don't want to answer that, tell me what happened to your nose and ribs. You're going to end up with two black eyes, you idiot."

"How'd you know I was the idiot?"

"Known you long enough."

"You tell me what happened then."

Corbet stared, and I pretended to be occupied with the IV in my arm, then he squeezed my shoulders, and bent down to rest his forehead against mine. It was uncomfortably intimate, but Corbet embraced physical connection, touched people when he spoke with them, punctuated talk with a wrist- or shoulder-touch, even an elbow-cup, and turned every handshake into a hug, his intimidating size guaranteeing complicity.

"What happened is your daughter died," he said. "I'm so fucking sorry."

I did not cry—tears were a waste and would leave me trying to blow clumps of snot out of my swollen nose—so I clenched my teeth and pawed at Corbet's back. He had no similar aversion to weeping and cried in deep guttural sobs. His tears wet my face.

"Someone walks in here, they'll think we're lovers."

Corbet slipped his lips to my ear. "You wish, white boy."

Standing up, Corbet wiped his eyes. "For a smart guy, you sure love to play dumb. I know you went to see those skinheads. Considerate of them to drive you back."

Had it been Joe who drove my car, Cerberus in the back seat, tongue lolling drool on the seats? Doubtful. Not Jessie, either. Or Leroy.

"My wallet?"

"It's there."

"Money?"

Penelope touched my arm. Was I really feeling her touch or imagining it? "Dad, you're not seriously asking about your money, are you?"

"No cash, cards were there, license."

"Not so bad."

Penelope's hand was still on me. I felt it as you'd feel any living hand, her palm warm.

"Death by skinhead?" Corbet said. "I can think of a few hundred ways that's better to die than at the hands of those idiots."

"I'm not trying to die."

"Could've fooled me."

"What do you want me to say?"

"Don't know. Cops'll be here soon."

"What?"

"Tell them you fell downstairs." He winked.

I tried to sit up but thick bands of pain tightened across my back and my head throbbed like a stress ball someone was pinching.

"I'm not pressing charges."

"Of course, not. Wouldn't expect you to be so rational."

"You know," I said and winced against a sharp stab in my lungs, "you don't get enough credit for being funny."

"Yeah, and you get too much for being smart."

A nurse in purple scrubs came in and Corbet stepped aside for her to check my vitals, ask how I was doing, etc., etc., and she was blonde and stout and nothing like Penelope, but she was young, early twenties, which meant she could've been my daughter's friend.

"Get yourself together, Dad," Penelope said.

"Try screaming at me again," I said.

"I'll do whatever I have to."

"Oh, yeah? How about coming back to life? Can you do that?"

"I can't save myself, Dad."

"But you can save me?"

Her touch was warming my skin, but could I touch her? And if I did, would it mean anything?

"No one else can see me or hear me. Just you."

"Because I'm crazy?"

She smiled at me like I were an adorable kitten nuzzling against her.

"I'm going to help you."

"How? Should I be like your mother and run away with some love cult?"

"You're too hard on her."

"I thought we were on the same page with Mom's 'crazies.' "

"Dad, she's mentally ill. Has been for a long time. We joked about it to cope with it, but it's not funny. Never has been."

Ellie calling out *Dad! Dad!* until I run into the kitchen to find Julie with a large carving knife in hand . . . chopping up every last piece of fruit and vegetable and meat. On the counter, heaps of carrots and celery and diced peppers and mounds of spinach and romaine and broccoli heads and piles of chopped bananas and pineapple and strawberries and fleshy clumps of chicken breast and sausage and pork chop. *Fuck're you doing?* I said. *Making dinner. What's it look like?*

"You should've helped her," Penelope said.

"She was never suicidal," I said. But was that true? She'd wake me in bed and whisper what I thought of as her Night Thoughts: *I can't sleep but I don't want to wake up; It would be better if I disappeared; I want the darkness to swallow me.*

But who doesn't fantasize about such things from time to time?

How about healthy, well-adjusted people?

"You can still help her, but you have to help yourself first."

"Hey." Corbet was shaking my shoulder. "You still with us?"

He was staring. The nurse was gone.

"What?"

"Off in La La Land?"

"No, I was . . ."

Penelope was gone, too.

Of course she was. She was dead. The only place she lived was in my mind.

"You were what?"

"I don't want to talk about it."

"Your lips were moving. The nurse didn't notice, but I did."

"I got a lot of things to think about."

"Talk to me about something."

"The easiest way to leave a room?"

"And you think I'm the comedian." Corbet hefted a heavy chair over to the bed, moving it as easily as a stool. He collapsed in the chair and exhaled forcefully, a sound of exhaustion and disappointment. It was one of his classroom mannerisms, part of the teacher's playbook for manipulating teenagers into doing their work. No one likes to be a disappointment, not even teenagers.

"Something *you* want to say?" I asked.

"Sure." Another exhale. "You missed your daughter's funeral. Hell, you walked out on it. You missed her burial."

I opened my mouth to say, *No, shit*, but the words stuck in my throat and I had to clamp down against the warm push behind my eyes. No tears.

Corbet wouldn't give me the decency, or the easy escape, of looking away. "You feel guilty because you couldn't protect her. I know that. No one could've done anything. But avoiding the pain is not the answer." He paused. "I saw her put in the ground. She was your daughter, but I loved her too. Like one of my own children. I was so angry and hurting, but I was *there*. Grieving. And what were you doing? Getting your ass beat by a bunch of pseudo-Nazis. You want to get hurt so bad I'll do it for you. Truth is, you're too scared to face the real pain. I get it. I do. What's a few bruises or broken bones compared to a child in a coffin?" He leaned forward. "Goddammit, you should've been there."

I wanted to scream. Punch the bed like a two-year-old in a tantrum. It wasn't fair. None of this was fair. Why was *my* daughter dead? Why did *I* have to deal with this? Why was it *my* fault *I* couldn't face the pain? Why was *I* a coward because *I* didn't want to see *my* baby girl put in the ground? Who the hell was Corbet to think he could reprimand me or give me advice? *Fuck him.*

I was breathing fast and it hurt but the pain was good, felt right to hurt, so I sucked in air harder.

Corbet stood. "I'm leaving. You can unclench your hands now."

My hands were fisted with tangles of sheet, skin as white as the fabric.

Chapter Seven

At some point, a woman in a grey business suit with straight, dark hair said she needed to ask me a few questions. "I'm here about your mental health."

I laughed. Couldn't help it.

She raised her pencil, steadied her clipboard, and wrote something.

"I'm fine."

She waited.

"Yeah, mentally, I mean. My daughter . . . She was killed. She's dead. Just buried today. Bunch of degenerate white supremacists . . ." Whatever else I was saying collapsed in invective-laced mumbles.

She kept waiting and then asked if I was married.

"My wife's indisposed."

"I understand," the woman said. "I'm very sorry for your loss."

I bit my tongue. If I didn't, I might start hacking laughs. That phrase—*sorry for your loss*—was one of those euphemistic sayings I opined about to my AP students. It's utterly inadequate, so castrated it's insulting. We say it because we recoil at the bluntness of telling a grieving father, *I'm sorry your daughter is dead.* To be honest, as my students say, I'd rather people say that and were real with me than phrase it like I'd misplaced or left something behind, a pair of sunglasses on a checkout counter.

"Before we discharge you, we want to be sure you're in a healthy mental state."

I nodded.

"You need to establish an approach for how you'll handle the stress of returning to your life. You need a—"

"A plan," I said, managing to bite back my laughter, even saying it calmly.

"Yes, exactly." She wrote something and stared at me again, expectantly. "Your plan?"

"Ah. You want my plan. Yes. Well, how long am I going to be here? I mean, can I go home tonight? Because if so, I have to think about my house, so completely dark and silent. Empty. We don't even have any pets. Maybe I should get one. That could be my plan. A cat. A dog. A hamster. A ferret. Something to keep me company. Something to listen to me. Can't talk to my daughter, after all. Not unless she becomes a ghost and haunts me. How silly would that be?"

The woman studied me.

I chanced a grin. She wrote something else, scribbled it out, *shaded* it out, the exact sound of Penelope's pencil shadowing white page into darkness. My brain squeezed. My molars throbbed.

"Stop."

"Excuse me?"

"That sound," saying it without opening my jaw. "Please stop. The pencil . . . it hurts."

She looked at her pencil. "I'll be right back."

She passed Penelope standing in the doorway. The big pink heart on her shirt taunted me with its Gandhi quote about love and life.

"What?" I challenged. "What do you want me to say?"

The blonde nurse from earlier returned with a syringe and didn't answer my repeated question until the syringe's contents injected into my IV.

"A mild sedative," she said.

So mild, in fact, I couldn't ask a follow-up question before I was out.

I slept dreamlessly.

Except . . .

Except someone stood over me. I felt them there, leaning down to whisper unheard words into my ear with little exhales of breath that chilled my skin.

Chapter Eight

Something occurred to me and I got out of bed.

The IV tugged me back and I hesitated only a moment before peeling the tape and yanking the needle. Blood beaded from the hole and I wadded napkins against it, bending my arm to keep them in place. It throbbed dully.

I almost went to the Nurses' Station but thought better, but they'd no doubt escort me back to my room.

To bed! To bed! Shakespeare yet again. Lady Macbeth in her fit of sleepwalking madness—her own version of Night Thoughts—when she can't scrub the invisible blood off her hands.

There was blood on my hands, too.

Corbet was right—I *was* guilty. Ellie asked me that morning to join her at the protest in town. *It'll be fun,* she said. *Then we can get pizza or something. Your treat.* And I said I was going to work on my novel. My fucking novel. You mean that sixty-three-page manuscript you've rewritten twelve times and you still don't know what comes next? Yeah, that novel.

But Corbet was also wrong. I *could've* done something. I could've protested with her, waving some poster board *Love Not Hate* sign or *Knowledge is Freedom,* and then I could've pushed her out of the way. Let the car hit me instead of me watching it hit her.

The hallway was deserted. I heard people in other rooms, saw TV light flickering on the polished floors, and smelled the antiseptic aroma of just-cleaned, but no one saw me in my hospital gown and socks walk out of my room.

I made it past several rooms before a woman in a red coat who looked both worried and distracted spotted me. She stood in a doorway and cinched the coat around her as if cold.

"To bed!" I said. "To bed!"

She stared, watching me go. I chuckled.

Two floors down was the ICU.

Nurses moved from one room to the next, their steps rubbery soft. Machines beeped, an old man moaned, and somewhere close, people were laughing.

I walked the U-shaped area, glancing in each room through the glass walls that made the patients look like subjects in a lab experiment—or animals in a zoo.

An elderly woman lay asleep, mouth agape, a cloud of grey hair thinning on the pillow. A middle-aged man in the next room sat forward beside the bed on which a heavily bandaged person gently moaned. An old man straining to stay standing with a walker squinted at me accusingly.

I made it almost all the way around before I found who I was looking for.

One meaty arm hung loose off the side of the bed. A large SS tattoo stamped his shoulder. Machines crowded the bed, and wires and tubes sprouted off his body. A urine bag hung off the side and the smell of shit wafted from beneath the sheets.

Logan Repp, aka Rando, had been hit a moment before the Dodge Charger, Midnight Edition, killed Penelope. Unlike my Penny Candy, Logan was not hit dead-on. He was clipped, spun sideways, smacking into other protestors, including Case (breaking her leg), and he might've come out all right with only a broken bone or two as well, except he whipped through the crowd like a spinning top and slammed into what was known as the Town Tree, a statue of a big oak in honor of one that was there when the town was founded.

His chest rose and fell in synch with the ventilator's sigh and hum. The blue tubes shook a little, stretching from the machine to the hole in Logan's trachea where a sticker on a connecting tube read, *Change on Sunday*. Beneath his lids, his eyes rolled.

"The doctors won't give me odds."

A sixty-something woman sat in a chair in the far corner. Her hands were joined as if in prayer. A large button on her blazer declared, BELIEVE!

"I was just passing through."

"So true of all of us," she said. "We don't know God's plan."

"This is your son?"

She bit her lip, pushed back the grief. "He's a good boy. Got lost along the way. The Devil is everywhere. He got so filled with hate."

A swollen crevasse scarred Logan's scalp from his right ear up and around his shaved head and down the other side. Metal staples glinted like gruesome teeth along the stitches. In black Sharpie on a piece of grey duct tape crudely stuck to his head: *No Bone.*

"They cut out a piece of his skull," she said. "Relieve the pressure. His brain is swelling. If he hadn't cracked his skull, he would've died."

"Lucky for him," I said.

"The piece of his skull is in his gut. For safe-keeping. Isn't that odd?"

"Like he's a mad scientist's incubator," I said.

She blinked several times.

"Frankenstein's monster," I said.

The woman shifted in the chair. "You're a patient?"

"Victim of an altercation. Like your son."

"Terrible, just terrible." She was shaking her head, tears glistening.

"At least you know he wasn't in on it," I said. "If he'd known the car was coming, he certainly wouldn't have been across the street screaming at the people who were chanting 'Love over Hate.' He would've stayed back, and watched it all with his fellow morons, like spectators at a football game. I have a question for you. What are you going to do when he dies?"

More blinking.

With the next automated breath, Logan "Rando" Repp coughed and his body jolted with the effort. Mucus rattled in the tube.

"Bacterial infection. Pneumonia, they think."

"So, he *is* going to die?"

"Who are you?"

I am vengeance, I almost said. But I was no superhero. I was just a man. A grieving father.

The woman closed her eyes, hands clutched even tighter, and she shook as if with a chill. She raised her arms, quivering. She was whispering a prayer.

I bent close to Logan's face. His breath was rotten. "You are going to die." I spoke loud enough for his mother to hear. "I will not live in a world where my daughter dies and you get to survive."

Logan's mother shook her clapped hands, a child begging for mercy.

If I felt any sympathy for her, I smothered it beneath my own pain.

"To bed. To bed." I stood straight and waited for her to look at me before saying the rest of the quote: "What's done can't be undone."

Penelope was standing in the hall.

I moved past her before she could speak.

CHAPTER NINE

I walked right out of the hospital.

My clothes were folded inside a plastic bag in the closet, so once more I was in the suit I'd been wearing since getting dressed for Penelope's funeral. It had dried in sweat-smelly wrinkles. I kept the hospital socks on and shoved my feet into my dress shoes where they throbbed.

On the bed and signed, my note written in all caps on a napkin: I LEFT.

I did not go home.

Part Two

"There are more things in heaven and earth, Horatio,
Than are dreamt of in your philosophy."
William Shakespeare

Chapter Ten

The town cemetery was on a back road, the iron fence so close to the road's white line you could snap off a side mirror if you were cruising by and got lazy with the wheel. A farmer's market with a Fresh Vegetables & More sign stood dark across the street.

I parked in their lot. If a cop drove by, I figured he'd be more suspicious of a car parked in the cemetery than in the little gravel lot across from it. *Except, isn't that exactly where a cop would expect someone to park who was trying to sneak into a graveyard at night?*

I'm not sneaking in. I'm paying respects to my daughter.

You mean the daughter whose funeral you walked out of and whose burial you missed because you were getting your ass handed to you by a mouth-breathing white supremacist?

"Yes," I said getting out of my car. "That's exactly the daughter I mean."

What would a cop say, anyway, if one happened to stop and find me in the graveyard? I wasn't out to desecrate anything, hadn't gone totally crazy and was carrying in a spade and shovel and a tarpaulin.

Your daughter was the one killed at the protest, the cop would say. *Goddamn shame.*

Yeah, I'd tell the cop. *I just left flowers at the memorial in town, as if there weren't already enough bouquets and teddy bears and posters. Then I wanted to come here and get drunk.*

The cop would nod. *I'd love to shoot those Nazi bastards myself.*

Can I help?

He'd laugh, tell me to call the police station when I was ready and he'd come back and drive me home.

That's probably *exactly* what would happen. A dead daughter is like a get-out-of-jail-free card.

See? You've been looking at this situation all wrong. You shouldn't be angry and trying to get revenge. You should be looking on the bright side. Think about all the sympathy you'll get. Free drinks and torn-up tickets. You can cash in on this for years!

I almost got back in my car. I didn't need to get drunk by Penelope's grave with such stupid thoughts badgering me until enough whiskey knocked me out. But Shakespeare urged me once more unto the breach, dear friend, and I approached.

The wrought iron spikes on the fence staves stretched long shadows across the street.

I'd hoped the cemetery would be closed, maybe padlocked. Or maybe there would be some skinny old man, coveralls sagging from sloped shoulders, his head like a warped and softening pumpkin, who limped across the grass, leaning on a gravestone to catch his breath every now and again, and when he finally reached the heavy metal gate, he'd size me up and down like the wizened old man in a teen slasher flick and say in a smoke-addled voice, *Graveyard's closed. Can't have you disturbing the dead, especially after dark.*

If such a person existed (a gravedigger? a groundskeeper? a caretaker?), he was nowhere in sight, and it didn't matter, anyway. The cemetery gate wasn't locked. I pushed it wide, hinges screeching a nerve-scraping, unoiled squeal.

The day's humidity had still not let up, and it weighted the air, thick and moist. Mosquitos and moths clouded the haze of the only security light affixed high above to a wooden post.

I crossed the street like the cliche of a bum, disheveled suit, uneven gait, and even a brown paper bag concealing a bottle of Hudson Whiskey. *I'm going to the cemetery and getting drunk,* I'd told the big, bearded guy at the register in the liquor store. I signed the credit card receipt, and he said, *Sounds like a plan.*

Indeed. *See,* I could tell that woman at the hospital, *I do have a plan.*

Except I didn't say anything because in my wallet I found a piece of paper that hadn't been there before.

It was the torn corner of lined paper, the flimsy sort from a notebook you buy for less than a dollar at the supermarket. On it, in purple pen, girlish handwriting with two little hearts as periods: *Stay away. I'm sorry.*

Mercedes.

She had written that note and tucked it into my wallet after stealing what cash I had, fifty or sixty bucks. And had she also driven me back to my house? My address was on my license, so that sounded plausible.

Why help me?

Maybe she could help me get revenge.

I hesitated at the open gate. The cemetery stretched over gentle hills toward dark woods, the graves like scattered teeth in some enormous pried-open mouth. Moonlight flickered through shredding clouds. That light made it look like there was fog rolling between the graves.

An owl hooted. A mosquito buzzed past my ear. Sweat sealed my shirt to my back.

"When shall we three meet again? In thunder, lightning, or in rain?" Trying for a witch voice. I entered the graveyard and spread my arms wide as if in grand welcome. "There is nothing serious in mortality. All is but toys!"

Macbeth says this after discovering the king has been slain but, of course, Macbeth is the one who did the slaying, and Macbeth's lines are irony or subterfuge or regret that eventually come back to haunt him.

So many things can haunt us.

"Penelope?"

Off in the woods, a coyote's human-like howling cry. Sounding pained. The perfect sound for the dead and decomposing.

My daughter was here, among the dead.

A metal sign declared there was NO SKATEBOARDING, BICYCLE RIDING, ROLLERBLADING, or SCOOTER RIDING permitted.

"Doesn't say no drinking." It was the sort of logic my students would use.

I uncapped the whiskey, downed three good swallows, the burn searing my throat and stomach, and started toward Penelope's grave.

The funeral director smoothed out a folded map on a long table in the funeral home showroom and pointed at several "desirable locations." I chose one near a tree because it sounded almost pleasant, and the funeral director gave me a well-practiced sympathy grin and told me it was an excellent decision. Then he walked me through the paperwork and tallied the bill for the burial plot, opening and closing the grave, the grave liner, the headstone (bronze? granite? marble? and the engraving), and the cemetery fee, and the funeral home processing fee. But wait, there's more—what about personalized funeral cards, or an engraved thumbprint pendant, or a glass paperweight with a lock of her hair inside it?

"Out, out, brief candle!" Quoting Macbeth again, this time his soliloquy after Lady Macbeth's suicide. I took another swallow of whiskey and kept walking. The tree was up ahead, a tall elm, moonlight wetting its leaves. "Tomorrow, and tomorrow, and tomorrow, creeps in this petty pace from day to day to the last syllable of recorded time, and all our yesterdays have lighted fools the way to dusty death."

I laughed and a chill prickled my spine.

Only crazy people laugh in a graveyard. Add that to the sign out front—No Laughing—a happy mouth inside a red circle with a slash through it.

Another swig of whiskey and my mouth felt puckered and raw, but it gave my legs strength.

There would be no stone at Penelope's grave. The funeral director (his preferred term, no 'mortician' or 'undertaker' he) promised the engraved marble stone would be properly set and leveled (at no additional cost, a complimentary service) once the stone was ready, in approximately two to six months.

In the stone's place was a temporary marker like those lawn signs that line the road and crowd medians during election season. Or like the sign we posted by our mailbox when Penelope finished high school: Proud Home of a Graduate!

What did this one say? Proud Resting Place of a Dead Girl?

"Life's but a walking shadow," I said in my best Kenneth Branagh. The voice didn't stick. "A poor player that struts and frets his hour upon the stage and then is heard no more. It is a tale told by an idiot, full of sound and fury, signifying nothing."

I was almost whispering that last line as I stopped beside a grave. I didn't want to look up, didn't want to see the fresh mound of dirt and the lawn sign with my daughter's years of birth and death.

Go home. Before you get too drunk to drive.

"Penelope? Is my Little Monster here?" Only an owl and a coyote. "How about my Penny Candy?" I looked around, spread my arms. "Your body is here. Why aren't you?"

Noth—

I heard an animal noise, a chuffing, snorting, grunting huff. Coming from something *big*.

I stood perfectly still, head down, and tried to peer up along my forehead, but the angle was too steep, the night too dark.

Whatever it was (bear? wolf? mountain lion?), I sensed its solidity, its weight, a living thing that might be several hundred pounds. Or if it wasn't that big, it had the strength of muscles layered upon muscles from a life of hunting and killing.

A snort and a huff.

Tricks of the mind. No different from seeing and hearing my dead daughter talk to me.

Except, why would I hallucinate some wild predator? Must be a Freudian explanation for that, trying to frighten myself away maybe, but I was too frozen-stiff scared for any such rationalization.

I raised my head and looked.

A creature, possibly a small bear, hunched near the elm beside Penelope's grave. Not a cub, but not yet a full-sized adult. Black bears were common in New York, and I'd encountered a few over the years, most notably one afternoon when I watched one knock over my garbage can and snout through my trash.

The bear was on all-fours and sniffing.

Pawing at the dirt.

Digging at my daughter's grave.

I forced my eyes to see it, whatever *it* was, which is as effective as forcing your ears to hear a whisper while standing beneath a blaring fire alarm. *You're hallucinating. Probably have a concussion from earlier. And you're drinking. And trying to summon your daughter's ghost.*

Too big to be a dog or coyote or wolf, and it didn't look quite like a bear, so a large deer maybe, but I didn't see any antlers. It was a moving shadow with bulk, and it seemed to change shape the way things do when the light is poor and the hour is late.

And the seer is losing his mind.

It didn't look like a bear so much as its shape suggested something ursine, and yet I also got the distinct impression of canine and even reptilian and, although ridiculous, also insectile. It certainly wasn't a crocodile—it had too much height—but I couldn't shake the idea that it might be as dangerous.

It's Macbeth's dagger of the mind, a false creation proceeding from the heat-oppressed brain.

Got my ass kicked by a skinhead and then got drugged in a hospital and now I'm drunk, too. Why? Because I'd witnessed my daughter's murder less than a week ago.

See? Explained.

That got me moving, slow but moving, toward Penelope's grave and the imaginary creature sniffing at her burial dirt. Digging at it.

It did not disappear like the witches Macbeth and Banquo encounter that vanish into thin air as breath into wind. The closer I got, my distance now maybe forty yards, thirty yards, twenty yards, the animal took on heavier permanence, a distant thing coming into focus.

I stopped and moonlight shimmered through the tattered edges of a passing cloud and then bathed the elm and Penelope's grave in bright glowing white.

What I saw was impossible.

It had four legs and a big head with a pronounced snout, but it was not a bear or a gator or a wolf or any other natural creature. Its body was thick and heavy, spotted with tufts of coarse dark fur that sprouted around a turtle-like shell encasing most of its back. *No, not a turtle's shell. A beetle's carapace.* It was dark and slick and gleamed moonlight as if oiled or oozing a mucus sheen. And the thing smelled. Like the putrescence of rotting meat, a stink so strong I tasted it in the back of my throat.

This thing was a mutation, *a mutant,* an experiment gone wrong that had escaped the lab.

It's just in your head. Only in your head.

It vibrated a snarling, throaty sound.

It was nosing at a lumped something. Another animal. A thing it killed. A coyote, maybe, but I couldn't be sure. How could I be sure of anything? This had to be a nightmare. I'd fallen asleep at my daughter's grave and my grief manifested into whatever the hell this thing was.

Except I felt the sharp pinch of my lungs trying to catch breath and the thick wetness of the air on my skin and the solid ground beneath my shoes. All my senses telling me this was no dream. This was really happening. And a crazed thought followed, *What if that dead something is not a coyote or a deer but is Penelope? What if this creature dug her up and was going to feast on her?*

Right there in the street, I collapsed onto my knees. Blood smeared Penelope's face and globs of it stained her shirt. Her waist was twisted unnaturally, one arm tucked around her head, the other stretched out as if for my touch. The concrete was so hot it was going to burn her skin. I smelled oil from the Dodge Charger. It had crashed into the metal poles outside the bank. The poles bent but did not break. No, the broken things were inside my daughter. The broken thing *was* my daughter. Looked like she'd been mauled by a monster, clothes ripped, flesh slashed. She wasn't moving. She was—*no, no, no*. Penelope's friend Case was screaming, clutching her leg. Not five feet away, a man in a White Power shirt, blood bubbling at his mouth, hand jittering, was looking at me. Alive. I stared back. Willed him to die. I refused to look down. Refused to see what happened to my child. Refused to accept this. Refused to believe in a world where my child would die and a hate-spewing asshole would live. *Die,* I demanded. *Die. Die.* Something touched me. Penelope's fingers.

Don't look don't look don't look.

The creature looked.

I was in the cemetery. My daughter was dead. Hell was empty and all the devils were here.

The creature's head turned into the light, and I saw its face. The head was wide and heavy. There was a fat nose and a pronounced snout out of which hooked fangs curved over lips dribbling saliva. Knots of fur clustered on its face. But none of that could dispel the idea that this was a bear, maybe diseased or ravaged in a fight with another animal.

It was the eyes that erased all other possibilities other than *im*possibility.

It had not two or three or four but a plethora of eyes. They covered its face. A cluster of them were stacked above the snout like a spider's, each reflecting the moonlight in unblinking, crescent slicks.

Cold fear iced through me exactly as it had when the Dodge Charger barreled through the middle of town, engine howling, and protestors screamed and scattered but Penelope was a second too slow and her body *thunk-cracked* against the bumper and rolled onto the windshield and roof, bouncing into the air, and *thumped* onto the street. I ran toward her as all around me the world exploded in a chaotic, horrified tumult. Those screams again, filling my head, louder and louder and—

I screamed.

It sounded completely crazed and inhuman.

The creature—monster, *monster*—considered me in whatever sort of brain it possessed and opened wide its mouth for a sound that was a coyote's caterwaul and a lion's growl and, somehow worst of all, a buzzing insectile whistle.

I couldn't breathe. Couldn't move.

It's going to kill me.

It turned back to Penelope's grave. Back to its kill. Sniffed, pawed at the dirt, carving a gutter, sniffed again, and began digging.

"Hey!" I yelled. *"HEY! STOP THAT!"*

Call it fatherly reflex.

Or a really stupid move.

The thing turned its entire body toward me. It was snarling a grinding hiss. The stench of rot was so much worse, a foul acidic stink.

It, whatever it was, was *impossible* and *had* to be a delusion. There was no other explanation. Except, of course, there was. Just ask The Bard of Avon: *There are more things in Heaven and earth than are dreamt of in your philosophy, eh, Horatio?*

It grunted, stomped the ground with one heavy clawed paw.

To scare off a bear, you were supposed to yell and scream and raise your arms and make yourself as large as possible. I'd already cut the distance by half before the part of my brain that still believed in self-preservation pointed out the obvious: this was no bear.

I tried to shout again, couldn't.

The thing *thumped* one heavy paw forward. The creature might weigh three or even four hundred pounds. I froze, but my gut was on fire, roiling hot acid, my mouth tasting of greasy pizza.

Not real. Not real. Not real.

It charged.

It might weigh closer to five-hundred pounds from the way the ground shook, but it moved fast as if it weighed only a quarter of that, a creature made of thick, springboard muscles. Moonlight slicked arcs across those bulging spider eyes, some large as baseballs, but all of them living and sentient. The mouth opened and it wasn't only hooked fangs in there. From either side of its tongue hinged out a double pair of long, serrated mandibles like those of beetles in the marshes of dense jungles. They vibrated against each other in a rapid chittering that made my teeth hurt. This thing (*MONSTER!*) was a child's deranged horror, a beast that hunted the black void of nightmares, twisting sweat-soaked sheets, and carving out screams into the night. It was a terrible, *wrong* thing that should not, could not, *DID NOT* exist.

And it was coming right for me.

It grunted and huffed, hefting all the enormity of its weight, and then clouds sheeted the moon and darkness enveloped the monster. So complete as if it had vanished.

Because it's not real. It's all in my—

The rushing immensity of the thing barreled right at me, and I was as dumbstruck as someone caught in the hypnotic trance of an oncoming train.

Notrealnotrealnotreal.

It might well have been a train, hard as it hit me.

A sideswipe, and I was flung to my right. My legs came off the ground and were parallel to my waist for a moment, and I thought, *That's not right,* and then I crashed into a gravestone.

The stone edge punched me just above my hip. An inch lower and the bone would've broken, maybe shattered.

I lay sprawled, my face smushed into the cool grass, the taste of dirt and blood in my mouth. *Don't move.*

It huffed and plodded back toward me. A growl vibrated in its throat. It sniffed at me. My heart beat so fast it felt like something under me instead of inside of me. My closed-in ribs were going to fracture and my heart would explode out of my chest.

Its snout—its mouth with all those teeth and those beetle mandibles—nudged me between my shoulder blades. If it decided to step on me, that would be that. My ribs would split easily as twigs and stab into my lungs and heart, and I would die in much the same way Penelope had, a monster crushing me instead of a Dodge Charger.

Then what? Eat me?

Warm drool dribbled onto my suit and seeped through to wet my skin. Again, I sensed the thing's weight, its solidity, its strength, but also something I couldn't quite identify. An ambiguous something. An otherworldly, spectral thing.

Ghosts don't have this much weight. Because this is not a ghost.

The monster prodded my back again with its snout and I wanted to scream, imagining its curved teeth so close to my flesh and all those hideous eyes mirroring me.

Another snorting gruff, and it headed away from me.

I felt unconsciousness threatening, but instead of welcoming it as you do when falling asleep at night, I fought against it, *tried* to stay awake. The thing—*monster*—was going back to Penelope's grave.

I heard it sniffing, then I heard it chewing, and then I heard it digging.

Then I heard nothing.

Chapter Eleven

My wife wasn't really in a cult. Or, I should say, what Julie was in, wasn't *yet* a cult. At least not in the Jonestown, Heaven's Gate, let's-all-surrender-personal-freedom-to-a-crazed-guru sort-of-way.

At least, I didn't think that's what it was.

Unlike the skinheads who festered in that dilapidated house on a backroad, Julie was in a gorgeously restored Victorian just up the hill from the middle of town. I parked at the curb and from there could almost see where Penelope had been killed and where flowers and teddy bears and homemade posters now comprised a memorial around that statue tree.

With the morning sun falling directly on it, the Victorian was a bright pink and blue, the ornate woodwork around the eaves elaborate like fancy icing on a cake. A sign on the front door read: WOMEN ONLY. And beneath in smaller, cursive text, *In a woman's heart is God's love.*

A large woman with a square face answered the door. *A bouncer.* She stepped out onto the porch, leaving the door ajar. I gave her room, and she crossed her arms over her draping blouse. "No men," she said.

"Julie Eden," I said slowly, over enunciating. "I need to see her. I am her—"

"No men," she repeated.

I nodded, glanced around, told myself, *Stay calm, keep yourself under control.* "She can come out here. I just want to talk to her."

The woman wore no makeup, her staring face fleshy and pale.

"Our daughter was killed five days ago. Yesterday was her funeral. I need to speak to my wife."

"I'm sorry for your loss, but we do not allow men to make demands of us."

"I'm not some controlling, abusive asshole. I won't try to take her from this place, whatever it is."

The woman shifted from one foot to the other, tightened her crossed arms. "What do you want?"

I hesitated. Good question.

I'd woken squinting into the sunrise, the morning dew dampening my clothes, and I'd stumbled to Penelope's grave where a temporary sign featured her picture and some innocuous prayer about being an angel. I expected either a completely undisturbed gravesite or a deep hole and an empty coffin fractured like a smashed boat against a rocky shoreline.

I found a small hole carved out of the ground, and I dropped to my knees and clawed at the dirt, first digging and then trying to fill the hole back in, a crazed reflex.

Sitting there, I listened to birds chirping and smelled the soil, sweet from the leaves and other things decomposing in it. *Not Penelope, certainly not her, not yet, not so soon.*

"There was no monster," I announced. If you say things loudly and with conviction, you might believe them. Then I wiped my soil-smeared hands on my pants, left the cemetery, and came here.

Why?

"I need you to leave," the woman said.

"How is she? How is Julie? How is my wife?"

The woman's demeanor softened, and she took in my wrinkled, sweat- and dirt-stained suit and the way I was trying not to lean on my right side where I'd hit the gravestone. And also my pair of black eyes and the metal splint taped on my nose.

"Do you know why God created woman?" she asked.

"You believe in that Genesis crap?"

She made a maybe yes/maybe no gesture.

"So, this is purely philosophical, not ecclesiastical?"

"God created woman not because Adam needed a plaything but because he needed to know love."

Someone was behind the door, listening.

"I appreciate the lesson, but—"

"You look like you're hurting quite badly."

"I've been hearing that a lot."

"In order for man to know love, however, he must be ready to receive it."

"How much sadder do I have to look to deserve love?" I said it like a joke but my ribs did that closing-in thing again, like some internal bolt was ratcheted tighter.

She said nothing, considering, and dropped her arms. "You have to love yourself first."

She turned to the door.

"Wait—" But I had nothing else to say. I didn't even know why I was here.

"Love comes first." The woman went back inside and I headed to my car. I felt jittery and exhausted. Why was I here?

I'd been seeing monsters, let's start there. Seeing monsters not because such things existed, not because what I thought I saw had even a remote possibility of being real, but because my daughter was dead and monsters had been crowding the brain. All the ones she drew in her sketchbooks, and all the ones who were real in human form, spewing hate and reveling in cruelty, *those* monsters. I'd watched them murder my daughter and then I'd been a coward and hadn't stayed at her funeral or been at her burial. *That's* why I saw what I saw. I came here because . . .

Denial is a river in Egypt?

"David!" Julie was calling out to me.

The woman was trying to barricade my wife at the open door, but Julie was reaching around the woman's head waving at me, like a desperate refugee begging to get on the next plane out of Hell.

"Hey," I said, hurrying back in a pained, uneven stagger. "Let her go."

"She's not being held against her will," the woman said.

"David! David!" Julie shouted.

I had to grab the railing to pull myself up the stairs. "I said let her go!"

"She's not being held—"

"Bullshit! Look what you're doing!"

My wife kept shouting for me even though I was only a few feet away. Her eyes were wide, frantic. Panicked and desperate.

"Let her out!"

The bouncer-woman relented and stepped aside, but she caught Julie's wrist and held her as she stretched toward me.

"Let go!" The anger felt good. Put all that jitteriness to work swelling muscles and deepening my voice.

Julie touched my cheek with her free hand as if about to kiss me. She looked hyper. Caught in a bout of the crazies. And I thought of Penelope asking me in the car after yet another hospital trip where Julie had to stay for observation and a psych eval: "Am I going to be like Mom?" "No, honey, that won't happen to you," I promised. But she insisted that "Schizophrenia hits in your twenties." "Mom's not schizophrenic." "Then what the fuck is she, Dad?" *Crazy,* I thought and didn't say.

"David," Julie said again, nose almost touching mine. "It's the most wonderful thing."

My heart *thunked*.

"Penelope visited me. She was here. She's okay."

I slumped back a step. "She *is* dead." I stared straight on into her wild, frantic gaze. "Our daughter *is dead. Penelope is dead!*"

She shook her head, hair whipping her face, a juvenile gesture, defiant. "Go see Mia."

"Who the hell is Mia?"

Her smile was a child with a secret. "She's across the river. Go see her. She has remedies. She can help you understand."

Julie meant the occultist woman in Beacon, a scam artist no doubt who presented herself as a mix of fortune teller, gypsy, and apothecary. More than a few times I'd thrown in the trash various suspect jars and cork-stopped vials of holistic remedies.

"No, I don't need anything. I'm living in reality."

Julie didn't scream or make that stupid child-like pouty face she often did when in these moods. Her smile, though, stretched too wide. She shouldn't be here at this self-help feminine-love cult for women or whatever it was. She should be in a psychiatric hospital.

"She was here. Penelope was here. She came to see me. She told me she's okay. She's safe. She said she loves us."

"You should leave," the bouncer-woman said.

"I'm going." I cut across the lawn to my car, grunting against the pain in my side. Against other pain, too.

"She said she visited you, too! In the kitchen, she spoke to you!"

I stopped.

Julie fully stretched, the bouncer gripping one arm, the other reaching for me, and now I thought of someone trying to grab a person dangling off a cliff. *Take my hand. I'll save you.*

"She said you were at her grave last night."

Gooseflesh hardened along my arms.

Penelope had been a newborn, crying all the time, hours and hours, no matter the bottle or the rocking or the swaddling or anything, and we'd take turns tending to her and when I'd return from my walk or my drive, Julie would be pale and sweaty and hold our screaming child at arms' length like some vile thing. "Take it!" Almost shaking our baby in front of me. *"Take it!"* I would take Penelope in my arms and glare at Julie. "Her! You mean, her!"

I turned, plodded back to the stairs.

Julie's smile was so large, so much like Penelope's at Christmas, toys all around, crumpled wrapping paper like drifts of snow. Julie's hair dangled around her face, making her look both younger and crazed.

"She came to see me. *Me!*"

Anger hardened the line of my jaw, the steely stare of my eyes, and the white-knuckled clench of my fists.

"No, she didn't. She's *dead.*"

Julie shook her head. She was wearing the same shirt as Penelope's friends at the funeral, bright pink, my daughter's face inside a big heart. "She said I didn't have to go to the funeral. She said she lives forever so the funeral would be a waste of time."

I could've hit her. Sounds awful, *is* awful, no question, but it's the truth. How dare my wife tell me anything about our daughter. Julie had been a mother in name and biology only. After giving birth, Julie had sunken into postpartum, surrendering to it willingly and gladly ("Take it! *Take it!*"), and in its grip she stayed, both physically couch-bound and mentally aloof, content to be miserable. She missed the milestones—the first day of school, the soccer matches, the frustrating homework sessions where Penelope cried at the dining room table that math was dumb and stupid and why did she have to do it, or the driving lessons, and the prom pictures, and the art shows where she stood before her paintings and sketches and spoke about her process like a professional artist, and the college acceptance email that finally came after the dream schools rejected her, and all the Friday movies with butter-drenched popcorn, and every hug and eye roll. *I* was the parent. *I* did it all. *I* deserved visits from Penelope, be they hallucinations or actual supernatural encounters. And if Penelope *had* visited Julie, had in fact told her it was *okay* she skipped the funeral, then the hell with Penelope, too.

I couldn't quite believe that last part.

Julie swallowed, tried to stretch down toward me but the bouncer pulled her back. "She said she forgives me! *She forgives me, David!*"

Heat flushed my cheeks.

If she were within range, I would've hit her. I'm not proud of that, and I'm not confessing it out of some moral righteousness to cleanse my conscience. As the saying goes, *It is what it is.*

"I'm glad." I sounded anything but. "I'm glad she forgives you. Because I *don't.*"

Chapter Twelve

Some nightmares evaporate with the morning's dew, some linger with you all day like a scab you pick at, and some hide behind a closed door, waiting for the best moment to pop out and say, *Boo!*

I was driving, going slow so I could pretend away the engine sound, and I saw the monster, a hulking thing, hefting across someone's front yard. I slammed the brakes. There it was: a bear with a pyramid of spider eyes on its head and a hard shell across its back and a mouth of hooked fangs and beetle mandibles.

An ice chunk fractured in my chest.

The monster was gone. Had never been there. A fat black dog trotted across the yard, tail wagging. Only a nightmare. What I saw last night was only a nightmare.

Tell yourself whatever you want, but nightmares don't sideswipe you into gravestones.

I'd been sleepwalking. I went to the cemetery, got drunk, passed out, and dreamed of that monster and—

You've never sleepwalked in your entire life.

"And I've never had a daughter die before, either," I said aloud.

What did you say about living in reality?

A car horn honked, and I jumped.

Another glance—only a dog—and I drove.

CHAPTER THIRTEEN

Corbet opened the front door of his home, eyed me up and down, and said, "Jesus."

He sat me at the kitchen table and poured a huge mug of black coffee.

"Thanks."

Bright sunshine filled the room, and the sounds of modern pop played from a radio on the counter.

Corbet stood opposite me across the round table. He was in jeans and a polo. "Should I ask why you're still wearing that suit and haven't showered or will you eventually get to that?"

"I spoke to Julie. I went there. To their cult base, or whatever."

"Uh-huh."

"I don't know what I was expecting . . ."

"And?"

I abandoned an effort to sip coffee. "I don't know why I went there."

"Sure, you do."

"No, I don't."

He took a breath, let it sigh out. "You came here because no matter what you want to think, you want me to push you to the truth. So, why did you go there?"

"No. There's something else." Dirt—*burial dirt*—crusted my fingernails. I picked at it.

"Gee, do I get to guess?" Corbet tapped his hand on the chair in front of me, same way he would to get a student's attention. "You look like complete shit."

"Thanks. I think I'm losing my mind."

I felt relief then, a big soothing wave of it washing over me. Yes. Like my wife, I'd come down with a case of the crazies. That was good. Perfect, in fact. A case of the crazies was much preferable to the alternative. *Oh, we've jumped back to bargaining,* the annoying voice in my head said. *It's okay to talk to ghosts and see monsters in graveyards because they're not real. You're just going crazy.*

"I went to the cemetery last night. Something happened."

"I know what you're going to say."

"No, you don't."

"Sure, I do. You went there, brought some booze with you, and you knelt at Penelope's grave and maybe you wept, at least I hope you did. Have you even cried yet? And I mean, really cried? But then, knowing you as I do, you probably saw her ghost." He laughed at my expression. "See? I know you."

Julie's exuberant voice, *She came to see me. Me!*

Upstairs, little feet were run-stomping around. Corbet had two kids, a son in middle school and a daughter not yet in kindergarten. His wife, Kelsy, was a branch manager at the Warrenville Bank. A beautiful family. Full of love and life.

Corbet tapped the chair again, his wedding ring making a hard knock sound. "Tell me about the ghost."

She said she forgives me! She forgives me, David!

"Not a ghost." I stopped picking my nails.

"What then?"

The moon's glaze on the hard shell, tufts of spiky black fur, ripples of dense muscles, hot drool on my back slipping from hooked fangs, and the beetle's mandibles and the spider eyes, so many eyes.

"Earth to Davey."

I willed my fingers to release the mug but then my hand was shaking enough for me to trap it in my lap. "There *is* a ghost. But there's something else, too."

"I think I need my own cup of coffee for whatever you're about to say."

He returned with a cup and sat, and above us little feet sprint-stomped the full length of the house. "Morning calisthenics." Corbet's gaze dropped from the ceiling to me. "So, a ghost?"

"Or a memory that seemed like a ghost."

"How literary."

I shook my head. "But that's not what I want to talk about."

Corbet made a show of slurping his coffee.

"You teach chemistry, but you took courses on zoology and entomology, right?"

Another exaggerated slurp.

"What about . . . weird creatures?"

Corbet started another slurp and paused, eyebrows raising.

"Natural mutations or something? You know anything about that?"

"What kind of mutation?"

A child's nightmare creation, I thought.

"You think a bear if it got infected with something or maybe drank toxic waste could develop extra eyes?"

"Like Blinky the Three-Eyed Fish from *The Simpsons*?"

"Is that possible?"

"You telling me you saw a three-eyed bear in the cemetery?"

"What if I did?"

I was staring at my hands like a scolded child, but I looked up then expecting Corbet's eyebrows to be so high they'd vanished or for him to slurp his coffee again, staring at me askance, wondering what size straitjacket would fit me.

But he didn't look like that at all.

"You went to Penelope's grave and saw something unnatural?"

"Yes."

"A mutated animal?"

"Yes."

Little legs thundered across the house.

"There is a branch of science that covers exactly what you're talking about. Cryptozoology."

"Seriously?"

"It's for studying such abnormalities, let's call them. Bigfoot, the Loch Ness Monster, the Jersey Devil, the Mul Lok."

I sighed but not because I thought he wasn't taking me seriously (maybe he was or maybe he thought I was coming down with the crazies), but because if the thing I saw really was in the same category as Bigfoot and the Yeti, then what hope was there for me to prove it to myself or to anyone else?

Might as well cross the river to the occultist woman and get a magic potion.

"What did you see exactly?"

This time, he did not slurp.

"An animal," I said, speaking slowly, measured, reciting the facts. "At first, I thought it was a deer or something, but it was big like a bear. And it was sniffing at Penelope's grave."

"What else?"

The shell, the teeth, all those hideous eyes.

"It was . . . digging up her grave. It'd killed something."

"You scared it away? Wait—it killed something?"

"A coyote, I think. Then it attacked me."

His eyebrows lifted again but he said nothing.

"It could've killed me. It broadsided me. Knocked me into a gravestone. I got the bruise to prove it."

He held up a palm to stop me from lifting my shirt. "You've got several bruises. Nothing unnatural required. You were drinking last night."

"Couple of sips."

"Uh-huh."

"I wouldn't believe me, either. But it's not the only thing. I've seen Penelope's ghost."

"Or the memory of her, you said."

"No. It was definitely her."

"Aren't you the guy who tells his students there are no absolutes? All things are relative? No universal truth? Nothing has meaning unless you let it have meaning? Anyone who is positive of anything is a—"

"Self-deluding idiot," I finished for him. "Yes."

"It hit you and then what?"

"It returned to Penelope's grave and started digging. I passed out."

Upstairs, the mad dasher raced again but thumped hard mid-sprint, sounding like a full-body sprawl. A breath's pause and the kid's cries vibrated along the ceiling.

Corbet stood.

"Finish that coffee and get cleaned up. We're going to the cemetery. Only way to know if you're losing your mind or not."

He headed upstairs to his crying kid.

My coffee tasted sour.

Chapter Fourteen

Corbet drove.

He took the long way, and I let him think I didn't notice.

"I'm going to say what I'm going to say and you're going to let me say it, okay?"

"You think I'm crazy."

"No. Maybe. But that's not what I want to say."

Even though I'd washed my face and combed my hair, my reflection in the passenger window was of a gaunt-looking man, gray hair falling uncombed, red-brown bruises darkening around both eyes that were bloodshot and staring out the proverbial thousand yards.

"I'm just going to say it."

"Like a Band-Aid." I touched the splint on my nose and flinched. "One, two, three, and rip it off."

"You need to let the anger go," Corbet said.

"Anger is all I have."

"It'll consume you. Eat you alive."

"So what?"

"Hate's a poison."

"One man's poison is another man's elixir."

"You're not funny. You're just an asshole."

I grinned. My cheeks hurt. "At least I'm not quoting Shakespeare."

"I'm not telling you to forgive those idiots. I'm saying to make your peace with it."

"How's that different from forgiveness?"

"Accept what happened, grieve, and figure out what's next."

"You think that's good advice for a man whose daughter was run over and killed and whose wife is a fucking schizophrenic?"

He hesitated. "There's no timeline on grief."

"You read that in a self-help book?"

"You want to know what I really think?"

"No."

Corbet's hands on the steering wheel were heavy rocks. The A/C blowing through the vents was making me shiver.

"I think whatever you saw at the cemetery is because you can't let go of the anger. Of your guilt. You want to blame someone. I get it. I do. Blame them all you want. But set it aside, you know. Don't keep feeding on it."

"Why not? What difference does it make? What difference does any of it make?"

"Oh, Christ, don't start on the meaninglessness of existence."

"Why not?"

"Because we're not college kids smoking pot."

"But it *is* meaningless." I punched the dashboard. That hurt too but felt good. "There's no purpose. No justice. No *rightness* to this life. It really is a tale told by an idiot, and it really signifies nothing."

We turned onto the road that led to the cemetery. Sunlight splashed the asphalt, turning it into the cover of a church bulletin, an angelic glaze promising salvation.

"Maybe I have eaten on the insane root," I said and chuckled. Hurt to do that, too.

Corbet pulled onto the shoulder and stopped, turned to me. "I'd do anything for you."

"Confessing your love?"

"I'm your friend. I want to help you."

"I know."

"Stop fucking around. You're going through a lot of shit, and I know you don't handle it well, no matter how much you want to pretend otherwise. Crack jokes, be a dick, all proud of your sarcasm, quote Shakespeare—*whatever*—just give me the respect to really listen to what I'm saying. Think you can do that, David?"

He'd never been so direct with me about our friendship, and it made me feel exposed and shamed. Male friendships are rarely so honest. At least not when the guys involved are sober.

"You're going to lose touch with your humanity," Corbet said. "I don't want that to happen."

The backs of my eyeballs were burning. My chest had sunken all the way in around my heart. All I had to do was let it out, all the goddamn pressure, the pain and grief and anger. He was right. I knew that. I may be an asshole, but I'm not an idiot. I was an English teacher. I taught teenagers all about thematic messages and character arcs. My theme was the danger of grief and my arc demanded I confront it. All very obvious. Corbet was my friend and he was trying to help me, and I hated him for it.

"Better to be a monster," I said slowly, even breaths, "than let one defeat you."

Chapter Fifteen

Two police cruisers blocked the cemetery entrance. Corbet parked across the street almost exactly where I had near the Fresh Vegetables & More sign. The stand was open, displays of produce outside and aproned employees moving around inside.

A uniformed officer stopped us at the gate.

"What's going on?" Corbet asked.

In the officer's quick appraisal, and in the roll of his shoulders, my thoughts flitted from headlines of police shootings to protest signs declaring Black Lives Matter to Penelope red-faced and fighting back tears as the kitchen counter became her lectern and she even beat her fist against it because it was so unfair so many people lived in perpetual fear of the police, getting so worked up she collapsed, sobbing.

"This is David Eden. His daughter was buried here yesterday."

The officer's expression changed instantly, and he was practically servile. His hand came off his belt, extended out to me for a handshake.

"I'm very sorry," he said, squeezing my hand. "Wish I could've been there to shoot the driver before . . ."

"Thank you."

Corbet gestured toward the cemetery. "Something happen?"

He led us through the gate and along the walkway until we could clearly see the giant elm near Penelope's grave. Three silhouettes stood in the bright sunshine. Two officers and one man leaning on a shovel.

The gravedigger.

The cop wished us well and shook my hand again. "Condolences," he said.

Walking at my side, Corbet asked what we were walking up to. "What I mean is, what're we about to find?"

A large bird flew overhead. Its shadow rippled across the gravestones.

"Were you straight with me about what happened here?"

"What's that mean?"

He pinched my elbow and we stopped. "I got your back. But be straight with me."

"Yeah. There was an animal. I thought it was going to kill me."

"Uh-huh."

The two cops had turned toward us, waiting. One was tall, his cap in his hand; the other was slender, her uniform bulky with the bulletproof vest.

The guy with the shovel was not the wizened old man with the softening pumpkin-shaped head I imagined. Instead, the groundskeeper (*gravedigger*) was a young guy in his late twenties with a scraggle of beard and wearing faded green coveralls.

"Help you, gentlemen?" the male cop asked.

The other cop's hand rested on her gun.

Shootout in a graveyard. Sounded like some dime store crime novel from the '40s, yet I could also see myself squatting behind a gravestone, gun in hand, peering. I'd never held a gun but I could almost feel the solidity of one in my hand right then. Not to shoot the cops, of course. Or even the nightmare creature.

I had other targets in mind.

Corbet introduced me again with the same result. The cops relaxed, became deferential, condolences and apologies and wishes they'd been there to shoot the asshole behind the wheel.

That made me think of the Harley with the shotgun. It hadn't been on the bike when I went back, so it must be in their house somewhere. I'd bet any amount of money they didn't have it locked up. Hell, it was probably on the coffee table with the empty cans of Bud and scattered white pride pamphlets. Now, my fantasy was a gritty '70s thriller where I sneaked into their house and snatched up their shotgun and before Jessie and his fellow idiots could do anything I was opening craters in their chests.

The female cop was staring at me.

"I must look pretty terrible," I said.

She shook her head but not convincingly.

"I don't know if you want to look at this," the male cop said.

"What is it?"

He hesitated. The other cop finished: "Looks like someone was messing with your daughter's grave. We found a bottle of whiskey and this."

They stepped aside and there was Penelope's grave with the temporary sign—her name, dates of birth and death, and her high school yearbook photo where she's in a black dress and holding a red rose to her chin—and the mound of fresh soil, except there was a big hole in the mound, and an eviscerated coyote lumped in that hole.

The monster had eaten the flesh off the coyote's face and most of its guts. What remained was strewn in a mess of bloody dirt.

It was real. The damn thing was real. Must've returned after I left this morning.

"You all right, sir?" the female cop asked. She reached toward me as if afraid I might faint.

Maybe I was about to.

"Don't worry," the other cop said. "Whoever did this didn't dig far. Your daughter's coffin—"

The female cop touched my arm and let go, as if sensing something unnatural about me. "Would you like to sit?"

"Normally," the gravedigger said, "I wouldn't've made a deal out of this, but considering the circumstances . . . I fixed the name marker, too. It was knocked over. Could've been the wind or an animal but the coyote . . ." He shrugged as if to say, *Who knows?*

"See," I said, my voice sounding far away to me. "I told you. That *thing* did this."

"What thing?" the female cop asked, hand going back to her gun.

"You were here?" the other one asked. He straightened, leaned toward me.

"Yes. I was here last night—"

"Those asshole white supremacists," Corbet said, cutting me off. His wide-eyed stare closed my mouth. "They did it."

"Wait," the male cop said, "you said you were here last night but you're saying . . ."

Corbet grabbed my elbow, steadied me. "He came here last night to pay his respects, but the Nazi dickwads who murdered his daughter must've come too. Probably followed him. Lucky something worse didn't happen."

The woods surrounding the cemetery did not look as dense and encroaching as they had last night. Few things are as scary in full sun as they are beneath starlight, and I could almost convince myself that whatever I saw here last night, whatever attacked me (*a mutated creature, a child's nightmare, a monster*) might well have been a hallucination or simply a real bear. My imagination had added the beetle shell and spider eyes.

Corbet gestured to the hole. "They did this."

"Why?"

"As an extra F-you, as a *warning.* "

"A warning?"

"You want to field this one, David?"

The cop was leaning so much he might stumble toward Corbet. The female cop was eyeing me.

"Your hands," she said.

"Huh?" I looked at them and then at her.

"They're dirty," she said.

Though I'd tried to clean myself up back at Corbet's, had even stained one of his hand towels with soil, dirt still crusted my fingernails.

I took a breath. "I came here last night, drank some bourbon. That bottle you found was mine. I got emotional. Went all Shakespearean. Threw myself there at my daughter's grave. Dramatic, I know. But I didn't dig that hole, and I certainly didn't maul that animal. Something, some*one,* else did."

The cops considered.

"Meaning the white supremacists?" the male cop asked.

"I went to see them. We had an altercation."

"What's that look like?"

I glanced toward the woods. Was it back there somewhere, that nightmare thing? Was it watching just out of sight, all those gleaming eyes, lying in wait in the shadows? "I threatened to kill them. They told me to never come back. I went back. They beat me up." A shrug, *Well, what did I think would happen?*

"I found him passed out in his car, right in his driveway," Corbet said. "They were considerate enough to drive him home. He was all bloody. I took him to the hospital."

I thought of the note from Mercedes, purple pen on notebook paper: *Stay away. I'm sorry.*

"Explains the black eyes," the female cop said.

The male cop clucked his tongue, glancing around, as if making a show of contemplation. "You're telling me a bunch of white supremacists beat you up and came here to desecrate your daughter's grave?"

"Surprised they didn't do something worse than dig a hole," Corbet said. "And whatever they did to this poor animal."

"It's bad enough," the cop said. "Something only the *depraved* do."

"I shouldn't have gone there," I said, though now that shotgun fantasy was taking on weight and the promise of possibility.

"These are the guys out on Pine Bush Road?"

"Yes."

The cops exchanged a glance.

"There's not much we can do," the female cop said. "We'll write up a report but first . . ."

"First," the other cop said, "we need to do a little investigating. Isn't that right?"

"That's procedure."

He was grinning when he asked us, "Care to come along?"

The gravedigger lifted the shovel and worked it beneath the coyote.

Chapter Sixteen

Corbet's smile was ear-to-ear as we trailed behind the police cruiser. The day was getting brighter, and splashes of sunlight smeared the windshield.

"I thought you said I should let my anger go."

"This isn't anger," he said. "This face is pure joy."

"Because of vengeance," I said.

"They're not going to execute them. They're going to give them a hard time." He turned on the radio, found a pop station. "Maybe I like the idea of cops hassling whitey for once."

"Whitey?"

His grin stretched even larger. "You should be happy about this. Isn't this why you went there in the first place? Why you walked out of your daughter's funeral? Why you got your ass beat?"

Stay away. I'm sorry.

What was about to happen? The cops would pester Jessie and whoever else was there, Leroy maybe, with questions about where they were last night, had they been to the cemetery, etc., and maybe Joe would be there and he would try to smooth talk his way into blaming *me* for this situation, and he might be successful because in a way I was responsible. The man who drove the Dodge Charger Midnight Edition that killed my daughter was in jail. The rest of the idiots had simply been exercising their constitutional right to public assembly.

Crimes against rationality, sanity, and civilized good will were not crimes at all.

It might feel good to watch a few of those idiots squirm and get pissy answering the cops' questions, but then what? They certainly weren't going to let it stand there. Couldn't let some pompous high school English teacher on summer vacation get the best of them.

Stay away. I'm sorry.

What about Mercedes? Maybe she'd come to her senses and ask for help and promise to testify against all those brutes she'd somehow fallen in with, and she'd go to a drug rehab, get clean and sober, and start taking night classes at Orange Community College, earn a B.A., get a job filing papers somewhere, data entry, maybe, and—

And nothing. Cause none of that was ever going to happen. I've had plenty of students over the years who could be lumped in the same category with Mercedes. Kids from troubled homes. Kids on drugs. Kids who chose the wrong friends. Throughout high school, they're all big talk and bullshit, blaming teachers for their failing grades and bragging how they're going to make it big doing . . . *something*. The grim reality that those ambiguous fantasies of fancy cars and fat wallets are damn near impossible dawns on the kids as graduation nears and then they're let free, as they longed to be, and end up in their parents' basement getting drunk and stoned and telling themselves they can still have that aggrandized future they fantasized even as every drink or hit seeps their motivation as it emboldens their delusions.

Mercedes's future was as nonexistent as Penelope's; she just didn't know it. Or she did and didn't care.

The cop car turned onto the road that wound around the development where I lived.

"Turn up here and take me home," I said.

"What?"

"*Home.* I want to go *home.*"

"They won't try anything. They'd be stupid to come after you. Doing this will *protect* you from them."

"You believe that?" In the passenger window reflection, my bruises looked like deep purply oil stains.

"You're going to deny yourself the pleasure," Corbet said. "You keep forgetting how well I know you. If you don't witness what's about to happen, you still won't have closure. No closure, no reason to let go of your anger. Anger is better than grief. I understand. You want to sit in your empty house and be angry. I don't blame you."

"Then take me home." I pointed at the road up ahead.

The car slowed.

"You think you're one of those stoics you admire so much, but that's bullshit. You're barely keeping yourself together."

"Which is why I need to go home."

He chuckled. I was being the petulant kid and pointing it out would only make my behavior worse. We tell ourselves we've matured a lot since high school but we just get better at hiding our adolescent selves.

"Fine, I'll take you home, but then I'm going. I want to watch what happens. You know why?"

"Cause fuck whitey?"

"Damn right. You remember that kid who shot up protestors in Wisconsin? He was walking around with one of those ARs and shooting people in the street. You remember what the cops did? *Nothing.* They let him walk around. Patrol. A brainwashed 17-year-old kid with an assault weapon. Irony is he shot white people. Jury found him innocent, too. You think a Black kid could get away with that?" Corbet turned into the development and sped up, though the speed limit was twenty-five. "I want to see the cops go at these guys because what's stopping those assholes from doing what that kid did? What's stopping them from taking to the streets or going house to house, murdering people in their homes?"

Stay away.

"Black people get upset because cops are murdering them. So, they march and maybe some get out of control and start vandalizing, and then the whole country battens down the hatches because they think the race war is on and they argue that the 17-year-old white kid with the assault weapon was only acting in self-defense."

I'm sorry.

"That's why I want to watch the cops give those fuckers a hard time. Because when the shit really hits the fan, who knows what those cops'll do? Will they protect me and my family, or will they look the other way when white folks go full-out vigilante?"

Most of the houses in the development were vinyl-sided bi-levels on quarter-acre-sized property built in the late seventies and early eighties, houses with two car garages and small kitchens, Tot Finder stickers on the windows of kids' bedrooms. That's something I could do, scrape the rescue sticker off Penelope's window. Should've done that years ago. Certainly no reason to keep it anymore.

"You go. Tell me what happens. Tell the cops there's a shotgun somewhere on the property, other guns, too, probably, maybe legal, maybe not. Maybe when it comes to white supremacists, legality doesn't matter. You think they got a lawyer on retainer?"

They wouldn't have a lawyer, not a local one, but Joe Klegg wasn't an idiot. He struck me as pretty smart, actually, smart the way most cult leaders are smart—they know how to control and manipulate others. As for the law, Joe would know enough to stop the cops from entertaining the house. *Not without a search warrant,* he'd say, calmly, Cerberus at his side, tail wagging. Cops question anyone else and it's those stupid five words again, *I have nothing to say.*

Corbet pulled into my driveway.

My house was like all the others except it was white and had columns out front. Donned in a Disney princess dress, Penelope would twirl among those columns as if she were entertaining guests at her castle.

"I'm coming back to check on you."

"I'm fine."

"You're up to something."

"I want to be alone."

"No, you don't."

"Better get going. You wouldn't want to miss whitey getting all pissy."

He started to respond but grinned really big instead.

Chapter Seventeen

"Penelope?"

The house was empty. I was alone.

In the kitchen, the bright morning sun that glazed the floor was gone and a diffuse light hazed the room like something in a dream.

"Penelope?"

I waited but again there was nothing. No ghost. No living memories like traps to snare me. Because that's all a ghost is, memory trapping you. Ghosts, as paranormal manifestations, aren't real, not beyond the convoluted mind that bears witness. If ghosts *were* real, we'd have tangible evidence.

She came to see me, Julie said. *Me!*

As if that meant something. Julie was far gone with the crazies, and I was, well, a bit crazy myself.

She said she visited you, too! In the kitchen, she spoke to you.

"Did you, Penelope? Did you speak to me? Were you really here?"

Maybe Penelope was visiting Julie again. Forgiving her. Telling her it was okay she'd been a shitty mom. Reassuring her that no matter how many birthdays she'd been in absentia, no matter how many days or weeks she'd been cocooned in bed, all weepy and depressive, no matter just how worthless she'd been as a mom it was okay because her dead daughter forgave her.

Where the fuck was my forgiveness?

I watched her die. *Watched* it happen.

"You forgive me? Huh?" My hand twitched, and I grabbed it with the other. "Forgive me!"

Nothing.

Penelope's ghost wasn't real, couldn't be real. Ghosts were bullshit.

"Prove me wrong. Go ahead. *Prove it!*"

The fridge made a clicking noise as the compressor turned on.

I took a breath, stopped, said fuck this, and headed upstairs.

Penelope's bedroom was at the opposite end of the hall from mine.

A wood-carved sign bore her name on the door. It'd been there since she was six or seven when we bought it at a craft fair. Throughout the years, the door had known a plethora of taped crayon drawings, a NO BOYS sign, and a stenciled grove of roses along the bottom that she later painted over.

I touched the doorknob.

"Like a Band-Aid," I said, same as I'd said to Corbet. "One, two, three, and—"

I opened the door, and a push of air passed over me. As if released from a sealed container—or from inside a coffin.

The skin on my neck tightened. *Hackles. Like on a beast or on a monster.*

Something was in here that I couldn't see. I felt it the same way you feel someone standing near you but just out of view, the way you sense someone reaching for you through a dark room. Probably that was bullshit, but it was just me so I could delude myself however I wanted.

Penelope?

I tested her name on my lips but couldn't vocalize it. Not here, not in her room. What if she didn't answer? She wouldn't, of course. Ghosts were nonsense.

Speak! I charge thee, speak!

"'Tis gone and will not answer."

Even whispered, my words sounded so loud in my daughter's bedroom, the room she'd slept in all her life, the room she played in, the room where we'd had so many conversations, from the quotidian to the morally complex ("What's the point of death, Dad?" a 10-year-old Penelope asked, or after one of Julie's episodes, "If God's real, why doesn't He heal Mommy?"), the room in which she spent hours sketching drawing after drawing, me sometimes watching from the doorway, her so zoned in she never noticed I was there.

If ever there was a place where Penelope's ghost might reside, it was right here.

Her name pushed along my tongue, but I couldn't say it.

Show me! I will be satisfied!

"Daddy, look." Penelope held out her sketchbook. She was on the stool at her art table, an adjustable drafting table Santa had brought her. Her legs dangled off the stool. The drawing was yet another boogeymonster, the shading so dark she might've used an entire pencil's worth of graphite. It birthed from that darkness, eyes like glass orbs, teeth sharp as serrated knives.

"Another little monster drawn by my Little Monster?"

How old was she when she grinned up at me? Ten? Fourteen? Eight? She's small, twig-armed, and then bigger, almost womanly, so much like her mother in complexion, right down to those freckles. And she was so close to the end of her life, her body twisted in the street, the air stinking of burning oil.

I love you. But that isn't what I said. No, I asked her, "Why all the monsters?"

"No different than people."

"People are monsters?"

She shook her head, all that red hair flopping. "Monsters are better."

I imagined a therapist's wood-paneled office, kids' toys scattered on the floor, Penelope's drawings splayed out on a coffee table, the therapist asking her where these creations came from, all these dark, terrible creatures. *Do you have nightmares? Are*

you scared at home? Do Mommy and Daddy make you scared?
And afterward the therapist clicking her pen and telling me,
Well-adjusted children don't clutter their lives with such horrors.

"Why would you think monsters are better than people?"

"They're protectors."

"I thought we needed protection *from* monsters."

That look then, the one of incredulity and near-exasperation,
a look so Penelope-perfect, so loving and so perfectly disbeliev-
ing. *Oh, you silly, silly man.*

I kneeled, caught her swinging feet. "Are you scared of something? I'll protect you."

"It's for when you're not there."

"I'll always be there for you. I'll always protect you. I
promise."

Her face was against the street, her eyes glazed. There was
so much blood. Streaks and splashes. I smelled oil and tasted
the acidic slick of bile. I was on the street on my knees and my
daughter was right there. Her fingers were touching mine. Still
alive. She opened her mouth and was gone.

"No!"

Stay, illusion!

As with any apparition in a Shakespearean play, mine did not
obey my commands. I was in my daughter's room all alone. She
was gone. Dead. Killed in the street on a hot summer day. I felt it
right then, the pressure inside me, not simply wanting to release
but about to.

"No." That one word, groaning in my throat, not even parting my lips to say it, but it kept that pressure within. Trapped. Good. Pressure was good. It gave me something to push against, to keep me strong.

There were no stuffed animals amassed on Penelope's bed, no princess rug on the floor, but there were still the glow-in-the-dark constellations on the ceiling through which winged unicorns were forever in flight, the colorful ribbons push-pinned around motivational quotes on the cork board (I blinked quickly away from that Gandhi quote about love and life) where her mortarboard hung with its sparkly letters declaring, Love You All!, next to the shelf on which a ceramic Cookie Monster jar kept its decades-long vigil between a Dracula mug crammed with pencils and a high-heeled shaped bottle of perfume, and her art award ribbons tacked to the wall between magazine pictures of Harry Styles and Taylor Swift and posters for *Toy Story 3* and *The Sound of Music* and my favorite, *Close Encounters of the Third Kind.*

I loved Richard Dreyfuss as the obsessed Roy Neary, and Penelope fell in love with him, too. How happy that made me. Stories shape how we see the world, and the stories we love in our youth stay with us forever. I'd make mashed potatoes almost every night so we could recreate the famous dinner scene. We'd each sculpt a heap of potatoes on our plate and take turns saying, Roy's line, *This means something*. For her 8th grade science fair, she made a model of Devils Tower with the mother spaceship floating above it. We were supposed to go out there, see the real mountain. We talked about it a lot and then we never mentioned it again.

Something was touching my neck. A trick of the mind. Or maybe it was Penelope trying to reassure me. But what if it *wasn't* Penelope? What if something *else* was here? Predatory demons, jealous of the living, torment them and then possess them, pure horror-movie fodder.

"More things in Heaven and Earth, Horatio?" My voice was unsteady, so much inside me trying to escape.

Beneath the window was the white chest that had once been her toy bin. Her name was painted along the side in bubbly rainbow letters.

Stay away. I'm sorry.

But I came up here for a reason.

It wasn't Mercedes' message specifically. It was the method of her delivery—the flimsy notebook paper, the purple pen, two little hearts for periods.

That's why I was up here. I was hunting a specific memory.

This means something.

I went to the toy chest, kneeled, a parishioner at the altar.

I opened the chest.

Her favorite stuffed animal, a plush unicorn, peered at me with its big plastic eyes. It was at least fifteen years old, the fur worn away in spots. *You should be with Penelope. You should be in her coffin.*

There were no other toys, only notebooks and sketchbooks and pads of paper and diaries with heart-shaped locks and a plastic container filled with markers and pens and paintbrushes. So many notebooks, from the cheap to the high-end, from dollar-store paper that tore under an eraser's slightest rub to vellum-grade as smooth as silk.

So many drawings, so many creations, a secret life. Why were they in this toy chest?

There was a small painting on canvas that looked like a self-portrait seen through melting glass. It made her look ethereal and terribly sad. I put it upside down on the floor.

I chose a notebook, flipped through it.

Small torn pieces of paper and a folded cocktail napkin fell out. Drawn in pencil on the napkin in stunning detail was a tree on a hill beneath a gleaming sun. Similar picturesque sketches were on the scraps of paper. Ellie was always drawing on napkins and envelopes and receipts and in-between columns in the daily newspaper.

I should've saved every scrap of her creations. Every last one. All those monsters.

On the actual notebook pages, pink and blue and orange doodles of cats and cartoon characters populated the margins. Happy creations. Not a monster to be found.

See? You were well-adjusted.

Tucked between the next pages was a gorgeous pencil drawing of Julie. Looked just like a photograph that'd never been taken, her skin so real I felt it along my fingertips. She was young and beautiful and happy. *Look, Daddy!* That's beautiful, honey. *Better than a monster?* You're the only monster I need, I said, and kissed the top of her head. *Is this what Mommy looked like? When? Before she got the crazies.*

I want Mommy to be better. I know, honey. I'm sorry. *Not for me,* she said, holding out the drawing. *For you. Take it. I made it for you.* No, honey, you keep it.

I dropped the notebook onto the others. That wasn't the memory I wanted.

Well, if you know what memory you want, then why are you looking for it? I'd come up here thinking I could commune with my daughter through her notebooks, but this felt wrong, invasive. If she wanted me to read any of this, she would've shown me. Just because she wasn't here to stop me didn't mean I should look.

Look, Daddy!

I picked up a black-covered sketchbook.

More pencil drawings. One was of her friend Cassidy, the eyes so realistic it was unnerving. Another was of Penelope as a little girl. The original picture was framed in the living room, Penelope at Hershey Park, her face flush with summer sweat, cotton candy gobbing her cheeks. Page after page of Princess Penelope, each dress and crown more elaborate than the previous. I hesitated on one of these, the snag of a memory (or a ghost) pulling at me, and was gone. Then I was staring at Devils Tower looming huge above a miniature Richard Dreyfuss. Small saucer-shaped spaceships hovered around it. Shaded perfectly, they looked right out of a 1950s sci-fi flick. She'd written at the bottom, *This means something*. And beneath that, *Do you believe?*

Was that question for me? Did I believe?

One more page, I thought, which would turn into one more and one more and I might be here in this spot forever. So be it. What's done can't be undone.

I turned the page—

My breath caught.

I wanted meaning. I wanted there to be a grand scheme, something organized by God or the Universe. I wanted a Great Plan in which we each play our part and not discover it was all some tale told by an idiot, not simply a life suffering the slings and arrows of outrageous fortune but one that actually held purpose, significance, meaning. We're all connected. There are no coincidences. I wanted desperately to believe that.

What I saw on that page was *exactly* what I'd seen in the cemetery.

Emerging from a crevice in shaded darkness, a hulking beast with spider eyes stacked above a wide snout full of hooked teeth and out of which stretched insect mandibles. *Princess Protector*, Penelope had written at the bottom. And beneath that, *Empty Devil (Dad would approve)*. It was dated two weeks ago. But was that two weeks ago she drew this thing or two weeks ago she added *Empty Devil*?

Did it matter?

Penelope had drawn this thing, and it had become real. Maybe she'd dreamed of it and drawn it. There was no denying it. She drew it, and now it was real. It really was a child's nightmare creation.

"This means something."

Except it didn't. I could force meaning all I wanted but this was pure coincidence. I had monsters on the brain and that's why I came up here. I wanted to confirm my own bout of the crazies. Penelope didn't draw a monster into existence. That was ridiculous. She didn't have superpowers. My imagination summoned that delusion and made me believe it. Stricken with grief, stumbling drunk through a cemetery, I'd brought forth that hideous thing because it could do what I'd failed to do.

It could protect my daughter.

Chapter Eighteen

I was sitting on the front porch steps when Corbet returned.

"Locked out?"

I turned my face into the sunlight.

"Still haven't showered, I see."

I'd stripped to undershirt, suit pants, and bare feet, but fully changing, never mind bathing, seemed too laborious. And unnecessary after what I'd discovered.

"They took the shotgun," Corbet said. "Gave a ticket. White boys got all pouty, but they didn't try anything. Kept saying they had nothing to say. Certainly didn't like that *I* was there watching."

"Surprised you didn't take video."

"You'll like this." Corbet blocked the sun so I'd open my eyes. "Some girl was there, strung-out. She asked if I was Ivan Drago. Told her I was a better Apollo Creed."

"Mercedes," I said, feeling a strange sort of grin forming on my lips. "That's her name."

A car drove past, a child's face pressed to the backseat passenger window. Was it the child's face or the engine sound making my eye twitch?

"They denied messing with the grave. Must've been an animal, like you said. Mutated or whatever. Who knows?"

"Right."

"A few hours ago you were hyped up about that but now you don't care?"

Penelope's sketchbook was inside on the kitchen table. Maybe I should show him. *Look,* I could say, pointing at it, *this is what I saw last night. Penelope's Princess Protector (Empty Devil). It was digging at her grave. It'd killed a coyote. It charged right at me. It was real. Her drawing became real.*

And what would my friend Corbet say in response? *Get in the car. I'll drive you to the nuthouse.*

"You think I did it? I got drunk and dug at her grave like some grief-stricken psycho? Think I mauled that coyote too?"

"What do you believe in?"

I closed my eyes. "Big Foot. UFOs. Richard Dreyfus."

"I know you think about it. You're a smart guy. But we don't ever talk about faith or God or the purpose of life or anything like that."

Across the street, a trio of young kids sprinted from one backyard to the next.

"You going to try to save me now?"

"No." He glanced at his hands, one scratching the other. "I'll tell you what I believe, though. My wife wants to think God has a plan. But if He does, it's one fucked-up mystery. I teach science so I'm not supposed to say this, but the crazy shit in this world don't make no sense. And, yes, I said that the way I meant to, Mr. English teacher. Screw your grammar. Your beautiful daughter is killed, and those assholes keep living. Life's not fair, right? Yeah, well, if Penelope can die while those morons live on, then I'm willing to believe anything, Bigfoot, Mothman, and alligators in the New York City sewers."

"Mothman, huh?"

"You want to tell me about this thing you saw?"

"Hallucination."

"Nah, I don't believe that. I don't believe *you* believe that."

"You know something, Corbet? You're really annoying."

"What you mean to say is, I'm a really considerate and wonderful friend."

Another car passed. It took a moment to unclench my jaw.

"Was Joe Klegg there? He has a husky named Cerberus."

"Didn't see a Cerberus. You should've been there. Might've given you closure."

"That easy, huh?" I sounded nastier than I intended.

Corbet didn't take the bait. He used yet another of his classroom tactics: the unblinking stare.

"Sorry. I hope those Nazi dicks were squirming."

"Got that right."

"You want me to stay with you a while? Order a pizza, get some beer?"

It sounded like a great idea, minus the pizza, and I almost said yes, but I shook my head, told him I'd be fine by myself.

"You sure?"

"Unless Cerberus shows up."

Chapter Nineteen

A few hours later, just past dusk, Joe Klegg drove up in a black truck. Cerberus watched from the passenger seat, the window fully open so he could attack if the notion took him. Or the command given.

I sensed his arrival. I don't have any special talent in that regard. I can't predict the future, but to one degree or another, most people have a sixth sense, an intuitive prognosticator that resides in the gut and stirs up the acid when you need to be warned. It's probably a survival mechanism, an evolutionary trick from our primitive cave-dwelling days. If Grog could sense when a predator was near, if his gut predicted it and he acted on that warning successfully, he'd live a little longer and thus increase the odds of passing on his genes.

And then, your child dies in a freak occurrence and you wonder why your prophetic gut hadn't warned you.

But I did. You were standing outside F&J's pizza when the protest was ramping up. You took your time eating two pepperoni slices and when you went out onto the sidewalk you even put your hand to your chest in the classic damn-heartburn-is-act-ing-up-again gesture, which was your excuse not to cross the street and join your daughter. That heartburn was *the warning. The Dodge Charger was already on the way.*

Could I have saved my daughter?

I was at the kitchen table, staring at Penelope's Princess Protector (*Empty Devil*), and I wondered with no exaggeration, or worry, if I was losing my mind. Getting the crazies, like Julie.

Better to go crazy than face the alternative.

Guilt.

"Dad, you have to join us."

"Oh, do I?"

"Depends," Penelope said, standing at the fridge as if in contemplation. "Do you care about doing what's right?"

"Ouch." This was last Saturday, the morning of the protest. I was at this same kitchen table reading *The New York Times*, and I made a show, slowly turning the extra-large page.

"Seriously, Dad. I know you think I'm a social warrior or whatever, but this matters."

"You always say that."

"Because it's always true!"

I chuckled.

She turned, hands on her hips, head cocked, hair falling across one shoulder. "What's so funny, old man?"

"You're my favorite daughter."

"Joke's a little old." She grinned. "Like you."

White letters on her black shirt declared: FIGHT EVIL. READ BOOKS. Just before heading to the protest (and to her death), she swapped that shirt for the Gandhi one.

After the monthslong debate in which community members tried to earn their fifteen seconds of online fame through impassioned public speeches before the Warrenville Town Board, the official ruling had come last week: a series of children's books about racial discrimination and American history—the vilified Critical Race Theory, as it was known—were to be removed from the town library shelves and indefinitely banned. They'd already been unanimously banned from the elementary school library.

"Dad, you're an English teacher, you should protest with us. You should *want* to."

"*High school* English teacher." I used my most pompous professorial voice. "I do not deign to read *children's* books."

"You're going to regret it when your AP students start talking about America as God's chosen country and white people as His emissaries."

"Missionaries, not emissaries."

"Whatever, Dad."

"How about Draculas?"

"No."

I tucked my upper lip against my teeth, spread my arms as if I were wearing a cape. "Vut do you mean, my Vittle Vonster? You can't help who you are!"

She did not even crack a smile. "We'll be there at noon. It would mean a lot *to me* if you joined us."

Instead, I got pizza.

I could tell myself I'd been about to cross the street and take up the cause for freedom of expression, but what difference did that make? I hadn't been there when it mattered. I was guilty.

The penciled monster glared up at me with all those eyes. Crescents of moonlight reflecting in them. Had to be real, didn't it? But no, couldn't be real, right?

I thought of that famous *Twilight Zone* episode where Shatner sees a creature on the wing of a plane and can't convince anyone it's real. The passengers think he's insane, and maybe he is, except in that final shot we see proof that he was right all along. *Proof.* Had there been paw prints in the dirt? There'd been a hole, a mutilated coyote. What more proof did I need?

That's when my gut did its precognitive thing and I got up with only a vague sense of what I was doing, and looked out the front windows.

The day was falling toward dusk, and the sun had passed over the house covering the front lawn in shadow. I saw the truck, Cerberus in the passenger seat, and Joe Klegg crossing through the shadow toward my front door.

Chapter Twenty

I was still unwashed in the same sweaty undershirt and wrinkled suit pants, which compared to Joe's short-sleeve button-down, clean jeans, and freshly gelled hair, might make one question who was the real degenerate here. There was no spiderweb tattoo on my elbow or Swastika under my collarbone if that clears up the confusion.

"Thought we could talk," he said.

"You want to discuss ethos?"

"How about the stages of grief?"

"I'm good with anger, thanks."

He grinned. His teeth were incredibly white and straight, his face handsome, American good-looking. "I'm here to apologize."

"I doubt that."

"David," he said and placed a hand over his chest, "I sincerely apologize."

"Saying 'I apologize' is not an apology. It's a semantic sidestep."

In the truck, Cerberus watched, tongue lolling.

"I want to offer a truce," Joe said. "Would you be open to such a proposition?"

"Why would either of us agree to a truce?"

"Remember what I told you? You need to forgive yourself."

"Thanks for the advice, but you're forgetting what I told you."

"Something about extermination, was it?"

"You want to threaten me or try to kill me right now, here on my front steps, go ahead. Otherwise, you can leave. No truce. This ends with my death or yours."

"Tanner Wyatt will be convicted for killing your daughter. He drove that car. There's no doubt of his guilt. He was doing what he believed was right. He was convinced of it."

"Yes," I said, "by *you*."

"And his lawyer will make that case. Poor Wyatt was brainwashed, inculcated by my hate speech and gospel of white supremacy and calls for violence."

"Sounds about right."

"He won't even be on trial for at least a year."

"What's your point, Joe?"

"You're blaming the wrong people for your daughter's death. Blame the crazed liberals. They're the ones indoctrinating."

"It's not my fault, it's his fault," I said in a crybaby voice. "He started it. Wahn. Wahn."

"In this case, you're right. They did start it. The liberals have staged a blatant attack on American values."

A car passed. My jaw hurt.

"That's why you wanted a bunch of children's books re-moved from the library? Protect the sanctity of this country? What about freedom of speech?"

"Traitors love to use that excuse," Joe said.

"My daughter, protesting against the censorship of some picture books, was a traitor?"

"The radical left wants to erase our history. They want to dictate how everyone thinks. They want to eradicate freedom. They claim they support free expression, except for anything *they* find offensive."

"But banning kids' books about Black people isn't because they're offensive to you?"

"No," he said, all white teeth. "It's because books like that are part of their insidious scheme. They've attacked academia at the highest levels. You can't teach anything with the N-word. Need 'trigger warnings' because you never know what's going to offend. You never know if a Black kid is going to accuse you of being racist or if a female will say you're a misogynist. Take that 1619 thing about slavery. Liberal crap to rewrite our history. All it does is give Blacks an excuse to keep underachieving."

While Jessie and Leroy could have fit in among my seniors who struggled with basic comprehension and essay writing but were bloated with quick rage, Joe might have been among those AP kids who harbored extremist beliefs, barely hiding their disdain for liberal views in their smug expressions and dismissive scoffs. I'd had a few such kids. Always white males.

A few years ago, I had a terrifically bright student who was an excellent writer, a composed and thorough thinker. During a girls' basketball match, a group of teens stole a tire off his car. The police knew exactly who had done it and brought him to the house where the perpetrators were trying to put the kid's tire on their own car. They were all Black kids who'd taken it. I overheard my student telling friends about the incident. He used the N-word, saying it with pure vitriol. Over and over. He became bitter, aggressive in class discussions and caustic in his writing.

"What happened to you, Joe? What made you like this? Random act of violence?"

He rubbed his hands together. "The largest mass lynching in this country was perpetrated against Italians. Did you know that?"

I smiled. "And how many Blacks have been lynched in this country? Two thousand? Four thousand? Ten thousand?"

Cerberus barked once.

"It's good to be the smart one in charge of a bunch of idiots," I said. "They idolize you. Do whatever you say. No one challenges you."

"You think you know about us? Read it on Wikipedia? I came here to offer peace. Educated man like yourself shouldn't be so quick to judge. Think you know me. You don't know anything."

"I know you're an asshole."

He nodded, glanced around as if scoping out my home, the property. "Americans *are* assholes. It's what sets us apart. It's what people like you, and your daughter, want to forget. Want to erase. You tear down a Confederate statue and you forget that statue was a testament to core American values."

"Slavery?"

He laughed, casually cracked his knuckles.

"You can get the cops to mess with us, harass us, get us arrested, briefly. Do that all you want. That's your right. Your freedom. But let me tell you about *my* freedom. I have a right to protect my interests. And when the police fail to protect my interests, to protect my freedom, I have a Constitutional right, a God-given right, to defend it, exactly as our forefathers did."

"The King of England is not a threat," I said.

"You know what makes Americans different?" Joe's gaze didn't falter as he spoke. He didn't even blink. "The rest of the world is full of crazy people, right? Violent people. You have religious fanatics who believe in stoning women in the street. Rape, abuse. Public decapitation. Child sex-trafficking. The worse things imaginable, right? They're violent, aggressive beasts. Wild animals. Those wild animals who do those things are scared of *us*. You know why? We don't have a code. We don't give a shit about some words in an ancient book. Or what some robed leader says. We don't give a fuck about culture in the way the rest of the world does. Like it's some sacred thing. We know God is on our side. And what matters is winning. What we care about is being the toughest, the strongest, the biggest motherfucker on the mountain. We will do everything in our power to keep our position.

"The rest of the world is scared of us because we will do anything to stay on top of that mountain. Doesn't matter. Those crazy religious fundamentalist terrorists are scared shitless of us because if you come after us, we will come at you with everything we got. It's not about a proportional response. It's about total annihilation. You fuck with us, you're done. We'll kill you and everyone in your whole family and your community and your country. We don't give a shit about God's judgement or the afterlife or other stupid superstitions. We will destroy you and piss on your charred fucking corpse.

"*That's* what it means to be an American."

Joe was psychotic. It wasn't about choice, not anymore. Whatever trapped him into this white-power-American-might mindset no longer mattered. He was its disciple. Spouting its hate in all directions. Maybe it was rhetorical strategy, but it amounted to the same. I couldn't blame him anymore than I could blame Julie for her crazies.

"What does any of that shit have to do with my daughter?"

"She was part of the liberal leftist Marxist terrorist agenda."

I burst out laughing. Couldn't stop myself. He'd come here calm and composed but I'd gotten under his skin, pushed him to the wall of his logic and pinned him there. He sounded like a total idiot.

"Go away, Joe."

"If you think you're safe, you better think again," he said and leaned in close enough for me to smell the mix of cigarette and mint on his breath. "You want to tell yourself we're a bunch of idiots, but we're more powerful than you think. More connected. We are the majority."

Another Cerberus bark.

I was turning away, ready to simply walk back inside, but I turned back and stabbed a finger at him. "Take your bullshit and shove it. All that crap led one of your followers to drive his fucking car into my daughter, so you can cut the shit now and get the fuck out of here. You want to threaten me? A promise to hurt me? Kill me? Let me ask you something, Joe. What the fuck do I care?"

We stared at each other.

He wanted to hit me. I saw it in his unblinking stare and in the clench of his shoulders.

"Go ahead, Joe. *Do it.*"

"Sorry about what happened to your daughter's grave. Wasn't us, of course. You'd *know* if we'd done anything."

"Yeah, you assholes burn crosses."

"Scottish clans used to set fire to the hillsides as a way to—"

"Who gives a shit, Joe?" More sweat slicked my back, and my mouth tasted like I'd been chewing on metal. "Let me ask you something. You told me Tanner Wyatt watched that Charlottesville video over and over, that he even said the guy who ran over Heather Heyer was a hero. You really expect me to believe you or anybody else had no idea Wyatt might attempt the same thing?"

He opened his mouth and grinned those white teeth again.

"Five words, right?" I said. "I have nothing to say. The white power creed. How noble. How courageous."

"I'll leave it up to you. Want to finish this like good, civilized white men? Name the time and place." He took in my property again. "Beautiful house you have, Mr. Eden. Good day."

He turned and headed back to his truck. Cerberus barked once more.

PART THREE

"Hell is empty and all the devils are here."
William Shakespeare

Chapter Twenty-One

Someone was in my bedroom.

An engine's scream had woken me in the night, or maybe it was the echoing memory of the protestors' screams as they fled. Or my own scream when I collapsed before my daughter.

I was on my side, the sheet pulled up to my head, and I willed my eyes to focus. The shadow person did not dissipate into the dark, and the back of my eyes squeezed painfully. My mouth swelled. Someone *was* there. Standing in my bedroom in the middle of the night. I was sure. Joe? Jimmied the lock and sneaked in? Or was it Penelope? A ghost I could talk to, maybe even touch, a thing to believe in?

Moonlight glowed around the silhouette.

"Joe?"

No response.

"Penelope?" I sounded small, scared.

Maybe it's the monster. The shape was clearly human but maybe the monster was a shapeshifter or some similar supernatural creature? Ridiculous, but if there's one universal truth about the middle of the night, it is this: all things ridiculous and nightmarish are possible.

The figure did not move.

I smelled something sharp, acidic, burning. Oil in the street. Blood in the air.

"Go away."

I snaked an arm toward the nightstand lamp. Searched for the damn knob.

Was that a whisper? The feeling of air displacing as the figure moved? Coming closer? About to attack?

I threw off the sheet, found the knob, and light cast away shadow.

No one there.

The moonlight streaming in from the back of the house flickered incredibly bright. *It's not moonlight.*

I was across the hall in seconds to peer out the windows into the backyard.

The ash tree was on fire.

***

It wasn't yet a full-out blaze. A discarded red plastic gas can lay off to the side, the stink of gasoline was strong enough to make my eyes water, but the fire was only beginning to stretch its yellowy-red fingers up the trunk.

I heard motorcycles, two or three, rev their engines and speed off down the street.

My neighbor's house was dark. The night was calm. The sky a blanket of stars.

A dream. This is too surreal to be anything but a dream.

Except the heat was too distinct, the smell too strong.

I moved as quickly as I could, unspooling the garden hose from the opposite corner of the yard and hurrying back toward the burning tree, only to curse myself for not turning on the spigot and then running back and forth one more time.

The bark, and the exposed places I'd dented with the homey sock, singed, but the hose worked better than I had any right to hope. I aimed the water at the base of the fire on the grass and around the trunk. If they'd spilled a can's worth of gas, I wouldn't be able to stop anything. Knowing those idiots, especially Jessie, he probably grabbed whatever can they had and didn't realize it was almost empty until he was sneaking in my backyard.

Thank God for idiots.

It took almost fifteen minutes to extinguish the flames and by then the air stunk of smoke. I had to stumble back to see it, but once I did, I saw how Jessie wasted whatever gas he had brought. Singed into the grass near the trunk, messy but unmistakable: FUCK YOU.

At least it was grammatically sound.

I was breathing heavily—*panic breaths*—yet my lungs felt too congested to breathe, or my ribs wouldn't let them inflate, and I collapsed in a patio chair. I dropped the hose. My hands were shaking. *They could've killed me. They could have fucking killed me.*

"Look, Daddy!"

My Little Ladybug, so small, sitting across from me, holding up her sketchbook. It looked impossibly huge in her little hands, like she was lifting an enormous canvas. On it, the ash tree done in impressive detail, the bark shaded into a thing I could touch. She was so young and so damn talented. I had no artistic talent whatsoever, and Julie's was limited to a few passable watercolors she'd done in college, so Penelope's skill was like a gift someone had bestowed upon her that I could pretend to take credit for.

"It's beautiful, honey."

She pointed at a small figure high in the branches. A little girl in a dress with long, curly hair. "That's me."

Before I could respond, she dropped the sketchbook on the table and ran to the tree and was scurrying her way up it with the impressive speed and dexterity of a little kid. She stood on the first thick branch and was now moving toward the next, already out of reach, and I hurried over.

She'd never done this before. Practically since she could walk, Penelope wanted to climb the tree, standing at the trunk and pointing high above, but even with my hands keeping her from falling she'd start crying and beg to be put back down. She once made it to that first strong branch before abandoning the attempt. "I'll keep you safe," I promised. "No." She walked away, wiping tears with her shirtsleeve.

But now she was high and climbing higher. "How far you going?" I was laughing, but I was scared too. If she fell . . . She'd been too scared to climb the tree and then she drew herself in the tree and she could climb it. A lesson even a child could comprehend. Finally higher than the house, she stopped and shielded her face from the sun, a captain at the prow, and gazed out across the vast world.

That was a memory I didn't know I'd forgotten.

"More things in heaven and earth." I swallowed something in my throat. My eyes were leaking but those weren't real tears. Blame the smoke. Anyway, what was I supposed to do? Draw a stick-figure of me beating the hell out of Joe and Jessie and the rest of his crew?

I should've left them alone.

What's done can't be undone. No shit.

What I needed to do was buy a bazooka and blow them all away in that shitty house. Or go there unarmed and goad them into beating me to death. Or get in my car and drive away from everything. Head out to Wyoming. Camp beneath Devils Tower, and then keep going west until I end up lost in the desert or I fall into the Pacific.

Penelope in front of a plate of sculpted mashed potatoes delivering Neary's line from *Close Encounters*: "This means something."

Please let that be true.

I went inside, but I didn't make it past the kitchen table where Penelope's sketchbook waited. I sat before it, set a hand upon it, and I guess you could say I prayed. I didn't talk to God, but I was filled with hope, and maybe that comes to the same.

Penelope was in the seat to my left.

"Summoning spirits, Dad?"

"More like little monsters."

"There's that Eden sense of humor again. You should really take it on the road, hit all the comedy clubs. It's the Grieving Father Comedy Show!"

"You're very funny."

"Learned it from you."

She was in that Gandhi-quote shirt again, her hair still damp from the last shower she would ever take.

"Do you have to wear that shirt? Can you choose something else or are you stuck in it for all eternity because that's what you were wearing when you died?"

Or was I imagining her this way because it hurt more? At least there wasn't any blood on it. Yet.

She offered her patented eye roll. "Being dead isn't like what you think. It's not cold and miserable and empty. It's just like life, actually, but different."

She made as if to touch my hand and then withdrew it.

Because she's not real. She's only in my head.

"Does it matter?" she asked. "If I'm really a ghost or just an illusion?"

"Delusion. Like Mom's damn crazies."

"You shouldn't be so hard on her."

"I'm not asking for marriage advice, Penny Candy."

"She wants to feel connected to you again."

"I don't care!" I slapped my hand down hard on her sketch-book. "You and your damn drawings. All your monsters." I opened the book so violently a page ripped, but I kept going, flipping pages until the Empty Devil (*Princess Protector*) was staring at me with all those enormous spider eyes, drool slipping off its mandibles. *"This!"* I lifted the sketchbook, shoved it in her face. I was shouting. *"What is this? What is it?"*

"It means something."

I threw the book. It smacked the wall and spit out papery innards.

Penelope was gone.

Yeah. She was in the ground.

Okay, fine. My daughter was dead. She was in a box in the ground. So, you know what? She didn't need any of those sketchbooks. Didn't need her pencils and erasers and brushes and whatever else she had. She'd never use them again. She didn't even need a room. She had a box.

I stormed up the stairs, down the hall, and swung her door open hard enough for the knob to dent the wall. On the ceiling, the green constellation lit the room in an alien light. If Penelope were real, if ghosts could actually do anything, she would stop me now. I seized the mug of pencils, a Dracula mug she'd spotted on the discount shelf at a home goods store years ago, *Look, Daddy!*, and I threw it across the room. It dented the wall and spewed out pencils. Then I was grabbing and throwing, snatching up and slamming down, arm-sweeping clear her desk, and punting her trashcan and my chest was as tight as a clenched fist and déjà vu tripped me sideways and I collapsed to a knee. I'd done this before. Stumbling in here after the hospital, Penelope's death a sour slick in my mouth, an acrid stink trapped in my nostrils, and I'd grabbed up all her sketchbooks and notebooks and threw them all around and kicked them and I screamed until I collapsed and passed out and when I woke in the morning, I crawled on all-fours, picking up the sketchbooks and hiding them in the toy chest, a coffin for them, too.

Penelope's quote board was right in front of me. I looked away from that damn Gandhi quote and was going to turn away completely, maybe even crawl out on my hands and knees before I could do anymore damage, but then I saw the other quote. It was an artist's credo, motivational and reassuring. But it was something more.

Create what you need.

Penelope was eight or nine (maybe younger, maybe older, so difficult now to be sure) and wanted to sleep outside, so I put a tent up in the backyard and even made a little rock-circle fire pit and we snuggled under a blanket before the fire beneath the stars and then she said, *Tell me a story, Daddy. About a beautiful princess named Penelope.*

And a hideous monster, I said. *One she must battle!*

Can we make it anything we want?

We can create anything. Whatever we need.

Make it big like a bear.

With eyes like a spider's, I said, *and a mouth like a beetle's but full of fangs.*

But she doesn't fight it, Penelope said.

Vut do you mean? She has to fight the monster.

No, Daddy. The monster protects the princess.

I'll protect you, honey. Always.

She patted my arm as if I were the child. *Monsters* are *always.*

I was alone again in my daughter's room, standing now at her window, the smoldering ash tree like an enormous ghost. I needed meaning. Purpose. A point to all of this, to life's joys and pains, to Julie's crazies, and to my daughter dead in the ground. It can't all be for nothing. *It must mean something.*

I knew what I wanted it to mean.

And what I was going to do.

CHAPTER TWENTY-TWO

Finally showered and shaved (the splint removed from my bruised nose), I dressed in clean cargo pants and a tee-shirt Penelope bought me for Father's Day. A Shakespeare quote emblazoned on it: *I would challenge you to a battle of the wits, but I see you are unarmed.*

The salesclerk at the Thruway Sporting Goods store in Walden looked at my shirt, read it, and asked what I was looking for—rifle or shotgun. The store was huge, selling everything you could need or want for any outdoor adventure, including lots and lots of firearms.

I shrugged. "Rifle?"

An image flashed in my mind of me as a Continental army soldier in a blue coat and tricorn hat, crouched behind a wall of stones and firing at British red coats.

"What're you using it for?" the clerk asked.

"Home defense?"

His smile was crooked but genuine. He sized me up instantly. Just another ignorant customer buying a weapon he'll never use because he's scared someone might stage a home invasion.

"Let's try a shotgun," he said.

After holding several shotguns, some with wooden stocks that made me think of cowboys and others that gleamed shiny metal like the Terminator robots, I chose a black Benelli 12 Gauge without knowing what the hell I should care about in a good firearm.

I imagined an elaborate background check, paperwork, fingerprinting, exhaustive questioning, a psych eval; instead, the clerk needed my license and my signature. The background check took fewer than five minutes.

"So, I cleared?"

"Absolutely. You want ammo?"

When I left, I had the shotgun, four boxes of birdshot, a cloth carrying case, a gun-cleaning kit, a pair of ballistic glasses, and a bag of reusable earplugs.

"Nice shirt, by the way."

I got in my car and sat there. The brand new Benelli shotgun was in the cloth case. The four boxes of birdshot and the rest of the items were in a white plastic bag on the seat.

"This is taking it a bit too far, isn't it?"

No one answered me. A man in a red flannel carrying an elaborate crossbow glanced at me and looked away.

Because I look insane. And now I have a shotgun.

What was to stop me from loading the gun and walking through the parking lot shooting people?

So, you don't just look insane, you really are.

"Maybe." I was petting the cloth case. "Maybe."

A woman walking by with her child maneuvered so her daughter was on the opposite side and together they proceeded quickly toward the store. The woman even threw a glance back over her shoulder to make sure I hadn't moved.

I could drive back to the house on Pine Bush Road and stand in the dirt yard with the shotgun and challenge Joe and Jessie and the rest to face me. Would they call the cops, or would they come out shooting? Corbet said the police had confiscated their shotgun, but they probably had others, illegal handguns tucked beneath mattresses, Glocks stashed in hidden safes with rubber-banded wads of money.

Or maybe that was giving them too much credit.

When in doubt, I'd tell my students, *procrastinate.* They'd chuckle. That good old Eden sense of humor again. *Or get help.* They'd wait for the punchline. *Go see your counselor.*

I wanted vengeance. Would that make everything better? Get blood on my hands, go to jail? Was that going to bring back my daughter? No, but that wasn't the point. The point was right and wrong. The point was justice. The point was, those assholes needed to pay with all they had. I wanted to be the clever hero in a crime noir who could mastermind a plan that would lure the bad guys into a trap.

But I was an English teacher with a dead daughter.

Who was going to help me?

Chapter Twenty-Three

The Newburgh-Beacon Bridge stretches across the Hudson River, and that day the water sparkled sharp glints of sunlight.

I parked on Main Street in Beacon and then had no idea where to go next. I could've Googled "occultist shop Beacon NY," but I strolled past storefronts instead. Coffee shops and restaurants and clothing stores and artist boutique shops. If I was meant to find the place, I would.

Oh, is that how it works? Was Penelope meant to die?

Don't people always say, *Everything happens for a reason?* God will never give you more than you can handle. Life gives you lemons, make lemonade. Look on the bright side. You have to look through the rain to see the rainbow. Life is not about waiting for the storm to pass; it's about learning to dance in the rain. You have to live every day like it's your last.

"Fuck you," I said, a couple glancing at me and hurrying on.

A car horn made me jump.

I was standing in the middle of the crosswalk, the light now green, the driver of a red Corolla gesturing for me to get out of the way.

"Which of you have done this?" I said in my best overdone Shakespearean voice. "His highness is not well."

He honked again, made an exasperated expression.

I gave him the finger. "I'm quite unmanned in folly!"

Then I was passing people who were drinking wine and dining on cheeseboards, and I imagined interrupting to ask if they knew where I could find the occultist shop where my crazy wife used to buy herbal remedies and foul-smelling potions.

Someone grabbed my arm.

It was a small, slender woman in gossamer layers, wrinkles creasing around two bloodshot eyes. Her grip was strong, gold and ruby rings on her fingers, her forefinger sheathed in silver like an elaborate splint. "You're looking for me." Her voice was crackly old. "I'm Mia."

If I could speak, I would've quoted the witches in *Macbeth*—*Where hast thou been, sister? Killing swine.*—but my throat was too tight to even make a sound.

"I smell your grief. And your pain." She sniffed at me. "Everyone gives off the stink of who they are."

I wanted to say something mean, to be an asshole, to wield my sarcasm as a blade, tell her she stank of incense and patchouli, and that must make her a dirty hippie, but no more words would come. I heard no sounds of people eating or cars driving by. The whole world was me and this woman. I was here for her at Julie's request and Mia found me. *That* meant something. Didn't it? I'd come here for answers. For counseling. For her to tell me I was supposed to get vengeance. That the gods or *the* God (or all the evil spirits in the world, no difference to me anymore) wanted me to spill blood.

"Double, double toil and trouble; fire burn and cauldron bubble."

I was suddenly cold. I pulled at her grip but she squeezed harder. Fear like an earthquaking tremble shook inside me. Not imaginary. Not exaggerated. I felt it. I was sure of it. My ribs were going to snap and shatter, my chest tearing wide in a gaping crevasse. My guts would pour out steaming right here on the sidewalk.

She was quoting Shakespeare, and I felt like I was dying.

No, not dying. *Being killed.*

Her old fingers trapped the blood in my veins. "By the pricking of my thumbs, something wicked this way comes. Open locks, whoever knocks." She grinned an ugly-toothed smile and then she was laughing, laughing, *laughing.*

I yanked from her grip, stumbled, hit a table. The world filled with sounds of people and cars. Someone asked if I was okay. I still heard her damn laughter. Her *cackling*. Mocking me. I pushed someone aside, threw my head left to right and back again.

Mia was gone.

Back in my car, I could finally speak. "Hello? *Hello?*"

No response.

"What was the point of that? What was that about?"

Nothing.

"Penelope!" I shouted it with everything I had. My throat burned, veins bulged at my temples. Ringing filled my ears. It wasn't enough. So much rage. I screamed. *"I'm sick with pain! I'm in pain!"*

I hugged myself. I was freezing, shaking. It was a while before I stopped.

My daughter did not appear. She didn't need to. I knew what she wanted me to do.

Chapter Twenty-Four

This time when the square-faced woman opened the door, on which a sign read WOMEN ONLY - *In a woman's heart is God's love.* I spoke before she could.

"I understand the no-men policy and wasn't planning on coming back here but I need to speak to my wife, please."

She considered, full body blocking the doorway, but she was looking at me with pity. "Do you believe in God?"

"I don't believe in fairy tales." *Only in monsters,* I added in my head.

The woman tensed and then took a long exhale. "Why are so many men resistant to know God's love, or any love for that matter?"

"I need to speak to my wife."

"What is our purpose?"

"What?"

"Our purpose. Our point for existing. The great meaning of it all."

"My wife. Please."

She shook her head. "No men. Have a good day."

Get the shotgun. Get it and show this bitch what's what.

"There is no purpose," I said. "No point to why we exist. No meaning. It's all random chance. We want to think we're special. There *has* to be meaning, right? Otherwise, why do we have such well-developed minds? Why can we contemplate our own mortality? Why aren't we more like primitive animals? I'll tell you why: Because evolution's a bitch. You want to believe in God, in the Garden of Eden, go ahead. Be delusional. I need to see my wife. *Now.*"

She shut the door but opened it again only a second later. There was Julie. Wearing the pink shirt with Penelope's face on it.

"David?" She had that far-away look in her eyes and I felt intense annoyance flare up because that look meant she was drifting into the crazies. "Such a beautiful day." She turned her face into the light. I used to think she was beautiful when she did that. Now, I wanted to grab her and shake her. *Come back to reality! Be normal! Be sane!*

"Have you seen Penelope?" My voice so tight it might snap.

"Of course. She was just here."

Get the gun. Get the gun.

"Good," I was barely moving my jaw. I stopped my hands from curling into fists. "I need you to do something for me."

"Yes, love bear."

She hadn't called me "love bear" since we were in that nauseating infatuation stage of dating all those years ago. We would sometimes lie in bed and hold each other, our noses touching, and we'd imagine our future. A beautiful house. Beautiful children. Tropical vacations. Growing old together.

"Penelope needs to tell me what to do."

Julie's smile got larger and then she finally looked at me. "Our daughter is very strong willed. You know as well as I do, you can't tell her what to do."

"Please."

She was looking at me curiously, and with Julie that meant a crapshoot for what she might say next. *There're tiny astronaut men in the bathroom sink,* or, *My soul keeps trying to peel free,* or, *It's easy to talk to the dead. They're all around us.*

"Forgive yourself, David. God forgives you. *I* forgive you."

Then she turned and the door closed.

Why had I come here? It's what Penelope wanted me to do. *Would've* wanted me to do. She couldn't want anything anymore. She was dead. So then why come here?

Because I wanted my wife to be the woman she was back when she'd sneak up behind me to wrap her arms around my chest and plant wet smooches on my neck just because. I wanted her to be the woman for whom I got down on a knee and promised to always love no matter what. I wanted her to be the wife who quoted movies with me as conversation, the mother who made funny faces at the dinner table until Penelope was spitting out her food with laughter. The woman before the crazies.

I wanted her to be *that* woman.

And I wanted to be the man who loved her.

Chapter Twenty-Five

Penelope was in my car.

"Crazies must be catching," I said as I shut myself inside.

With the windows up and the A/C off, the car was a hotbox. I didn't care. Let it stifle me. On a hot day, the inside of a car can reach over 150 degrees. Easily enough to kill an animal or small child. What about an adult? Maybe I could just sit in this oven and let that be that.

"To be or not to be?" Penelope asked.

She was right there in the passenger seat, as complete and solid as she had been in life. So young and yet looking so adult. It hurt. There was no relief, no hope. Ghost or delusion didn't matter—my daughter was dead.

"I need to know what to do."

"You mean with this?" She spread her hands over her lap like a jeweler displaying merchandise and there was the shotgun in its cloth case.

"Yes." My voice sounded small. "I'll return it. Right now. Just tell me."

"Dad, remember what you said about my art after I didn't get into art school?"

"I believe I said, 'Fuck those idiots.' "

Cue: Penelope eye roll. "Not about them, Dad. About me. About my art."

There I was standing in her bedroom doorway, she cross-legged on the bed, head down, the rejection in her lap. She sniffed back fresh tears. My heart broke for her and I wanted to scream damnation at the cruel fools who rejected my beautiful daughter, but that's not what she needed.

"I told you, 'Use it.' "

"Yes, and that's what I'm telling you to do. *Use it.* But not this."

"Then what?"

But she didn't need to say. "Is it real? The monster? Are you?"

She slouched in the seat and propped her bare feet on the dashboard, her toenails polished pink. "Does it matter?"

"Of course it—"

She was gone.

Chapter Twenty-Six

Mercedes was sitting on my front porch. Cerberus was obediently beside her, tongue sagging. His leash lay pooled beside him.

The car really was a hotbox, and now I was wet with fresh sweat that gave me a rash of chills. Could intense heat bring on hallucinations? Did it matter?

She was picking at her nails and dressed in baggy jean shorts and a crop top. She looked like she was only fourteen, lanky and too skinny, too pale, brown no-sleep smudges under her eyes. Not that I should judge with my double black eyes.

"I was about to head your way. You've saved me a trip. I have a message for Joe."

Cerberus adjusted his paws and stood straighter, tail wagging. "They set fire to your tree. They'll do worse. Please leave them alone. I'm sorry." She sounded clearer than her fogged expression. Maybe she was clean, for now anyway.

"Was it Jessie? Leroy? They were here, right? I heard the motorcycles."

"I left you a note. They'll kill you, you know."

"I appreciate the warning." But I've got *shotguns and monsters,* I thought.

Cerberus fidgeted his paws again and whined. I petted him.

"I knew your daughter," she said, petting Cerberus at the same time. "We weren't friends or anything. I saw her around town. She was always happy. This house. You for a dad. Like some perfect movie."

"What about your parents?"

She laughed in a terribly sad way. "They don't care."

"I'm sure they do."

"They have a funny way of showing it. Kick me out. Ignore me. Like, I know I'm not some perfect A-student goody-good or whatever, but it's not my fault. You know?"

"Where do they live?"

She looked up at me. "I didn't come here to be saved. I wanted to say I'm sorry for what they did, what they've done, and I don't want anything worse to happen."

She stood and I took her hand. She looked shocked.

"Let me help you."

She didn't respond, perhaps surprised a man could touch her without hurting her. Or maybe it amounted to the same—men touching her in whatever way they wanted. Maybe she feared I was about to proposition her. I let go. "You don't have to go back there."

"I wish they would all disappear, you know? Like I could be that kid in the movie who wakes up, his family is gone, and he thinks he wished them away. How stupid."

"It isn't. But wishing won't work. You have to take action. You have to leave."

"They're all I have."

"They're ugly men. Poison men."

She took up Cerberus's leash. He trotted down the steps.

"Will you do something for me?"

She waited.

"Tell Joe I want to put an end to this. I'll be at the cemetery tonight at midnight. He can come here and burn my house down if he wants, but he doesn't need to be so dramatic. Tell him we can finish this like good, civilized *white men*. Tonight. The cemetery. Midnight."

"You don't want to do that," she said.

"Will you tell him?"

"I'm really sorry for what happened to your daughter. It's not fair. Life is bullshit." She walked a few steps and stopped. "You're right. Joe's poison. They all are. It's like those labels that say, Caution - Do Not Eat. But it's too late, I've eaten it."

She headed toward the driveway, me too dumbstruck to say anything.

"It's not too late," I finally said.

Another stop and turn. "I'm teaching Cerberus a new trick. I want him to bite Joe in the balls. Or in his pretty face. Or both."

She smiled, seemingly fantasizing, and walked down the driveway and into the street.

When she was out of view, I got the shotgun from my car. Though it was in its cloth case, anyone watching would recognize immediately what I was holding. I felt exposed and looked around as if expecting neighbors peering around window curtains or a teenager passing on a bike snapping a cellphone shot.

The bullets were gone. Not in the footwell or under the seat or in the back. All gone.

Use it, Penelope said. *But not this.*

She'd spread her hands over the gun as if displaying merchandise, but really she'd been a magician presenting an illusion. *Now you see it, now you don't.*

Chapter Twenty-Seven

"I need your help," I told Corbet when he answered his phone.

"With what?"

"Are you still willing to believe anything?"

"Whatever you got."

"You keep chemicals in your classroom, right?"

"What's going on in that head of yours?"

"Come pick me up. And, oh yeah, bring a shovel."

"Why?"

"For digging."

I told him the plan.

Turned out, we didn't have to go to the school. All the toxic chemicals you'd ever need are already in your house.

He's poison, Mercedes said.

Chapter Twenty-Eight

Julie's crazies were bad enough for me to take her to the hospital on several occasions and one time I had to call an ambulance. She'd been in a cleaning frenzy. Dusting, sweeping, vacuuming, polishing, Clorox-ing, Drano-ing, scrubbing, scrubbing, scrubbing. The bathroom tile wasn't white enough, she said. She went at it with bleach. Tons of it. Then she added ammonia. I found her passed out on the floor, the room stinking so bad I might have passed out as well if I hadn't dragged her out of there immediately. Twin leg trails of cleaning fluid reached all the way out onto the front porch. The paramedics said her lungs were filling with fluid.

"It's a good way to die," Corbet said to me at the hospital. "Mix bleach with ammonia and you get chloramine vapor. Toxic. Burns the eyes and nose and throat and restricts breathing. It can be deadly and very quick."

I threw out the bleach and the ammonia. But I didn't throw out everything. In the garage, stashed way in the back behind a rusted toolbox, I found what I needed.

I dusted it off and grinned.

His pretty face, I thought.

Chapter Twenty-Nine

"You think he'll show?" Corbet asked.

"He'll show," I said.

Midnight was hours off, but the last of the sun's red-and-gold splashes were melting down the sky. You could almost pretend it wasn't a graveyard we were looking at but some natural formation of sculpted rocks where ancient civilizations conducted rituals to the gods.

Poetic or insane? *Does it matter?*

"This is crazy. You know that, right?"

"You're going to be fine," I said.

"And I'm supposed to let you maybe get killed?"

"I'll be fine, too."

A car drove past and my hands tensed on the wheel.

"Oh, sure, that's why we're parked outside a cemetery with a shotgun, a couple shovels, and a bottle of drain cleaner. Because *you're* fine. Right as rain."

"Do I detect sarcasm?"

"No, no, of course not."

"I thought *I* was the asshole in this friendship."

"You're good at bringing it out in others," Corbet said.

"I probably should've been nicer to the white supremacists who killed my daughter."

"My mother always said you should kill people with kindness," Corbet said.

We almost laughed then; you could feel the potential for it, but then I was thinking of how kind Penelope always was. She would make me give spare change to the guy at the highway exit ramp who stood there with a cardboard sign. She would ask old women in the grocery store if they needed help. She'd sit with Mom at the dining room table when Julie was locked in one of her mute phases and talk in the soothing voice you use with a frightened kitten. She never gave up asking me to join her in the street and hold up a sign. She believed I could be a better man.

So much for laughing.

Chapter Thirty

Penelope stared up at me, those red curls dangling, her small hand tugging on my pant leg. How old was she? Five? Fifteen? It was especially cruel that I wasn't sure.

"Yes, honey?"

She mouthed something but what came out was the monstrous howl of a 1977 Dodge Charger, Midnight Edition.

———

A tractor-trailer barreling past woke me.

"Whoa," Corbet said, grabbing my arm. "You're okay."

I didn't believe him. It was almost midnight and we were outside a cemetery. The only light out here was a security lamp high on a post. Bugs swarmed its halo, and its light cast the cemetery entrance in sickly yellow. This was not a place where anyone was "okay."

"Let's set up," I said.

"Set the bait, you mean?"

"That's exactly what I mean."

In addition to the other supplies, we also had flashlights. Mine was a small plastic thing that fit in a pocket, but Corbet had one of those big silver Maglites with a beam that shoves the dark away fifty feet.

We made our way up the hill toward the elm.

The night was humid and smelled sweet.

The gravestones here were newer, some reflectively shiny. The older stones were farther back, shrouded in the night, but one day even these shiny ones would become faded and slanted and weatherworn and casual strollers would comment that one had four children or this one almost hit a hundred or that girl was only nineteen, how sad.

"Why are we doing this?"

Either of us could have asked that, yet I was surprised to hear it come from me.

Corbet shone the flashlight directly into my face, blinding me for a moment before taking it away. "Really? You're asking that now? You're holding a shotgun in a cemetery at midnight and you're asking that now?"

"No bullets."

He stopped, breathed out. "Be real with me right now. What do you want to do?"

I took a step and fell to one knee.

You know that phrase, *overcome with emotion*? It's the sort of hollow cliche that gives nothing to a reader. I advised my AP students to avoid such lazy writing. *Give the reader experiences, not shorthand.*

But here's the thing, in that moment with my best friend staring at me in a graveyard where my only child was buried, I knew what it meant to be overcome with emotion. I understood then why the phrase existed, why it's more merciful to write that than to describe how the quivering in my gut pushed out through all my limbs, palsied them, and how when I tried to speak the words were there but jumbled and mushed together and my ribs squeezed out a single throat-scraper, the wailing cry of a survivor on a blood-soaked battlefield, and I sobbed hurt from a place no one could reach. That's what it meant to be overcome with emotion.

Corbet hoisted me into a hug. "Cry, you bastard. Do it."

I couldn't. Not yet.

Chapter Thirty-One

Corbet went along with the whole thing and was in position when Joe's truck pulled into the open cemetery entrance. He left the headlights on as the doors opened and men got out.

Beside Penelope's burial plot, I stood, the giant elm's trunk like an ancient monolith, the night sky stretching infinitely above me with its millions and millions of pinpoint stars. I thought of the glowing green stars on the ceiling above Penelope's bed in which winged unicorns also flew. *You think there really is alien life?* she asked while shoveling popcorn in her mouth as we watched Richard Dreyfus sneak up Devils Tower. *Look in the mirror,* I said. *Real funny, Dad.*

"Hey!" It was Joe. He was coming up the hill, Jessie on his right, Erik on his left. Leroy lumbered behind. Even if he made it up here, he'd be completely out of breath. "Hey!" Joe said again, and Cerberus barked once.

I waited until they were closer before responding.

"You're supposed to say, 'Turn hellhound, turn!' Or maybe I'm the one who's supposed to say that, depends on your perspective."

"You wanted us here," Joe said, "and now we're here."

"No hoods? No burning cross?"

"You want to put an end to this. What do you propose?"

I pretended to contemplate.

All four men were wearing black boots with red laces, jeans, and white tank top undershirts. The white supremacist's uniform. Joe was the only one with more than a shaved-head prickle of hair, and he also wore a pair of red suspenders, symbolizing something in their ridiculous hate culture but which made him look like a character from *Guys and Dolls*.

I saw no weapons other than my wool sock with the taped billiard ball inside. Jessie held it up, let it rock side to side.

Tick, tick, tick, tick. I saw myself cross-legged before the grandfather clock, counting the seconds as the pendulum swung, and as I had the other morning, I clucked my tongue to the beat. *Tick, tick, tick, tick.*

"He's crazy," Jessie said. "Let me do him and be done."

"Shut up, Jessie," Erik said and glanced at Joe, unsure but willing enough for anything.

"What stage of grief is this?" Joe gestured to all the graves. "Have we finally reached acceptance?"

"Yes, I think I have."

"Wonderful."

"I've accepted what must be done. And once it's done, it can't be undone." He was staring at me curiously. Leashed beside him, Cerberus sat patiently. "I've accepted that you and your fellow morons need to die."

"Your move," Joe said, calm as ever.

Screw your courage to the sticking place, I told myself. "You remember when that asshole shot up the church in Charleston?"

"Dylan Roof," Joe said.

"Fuck his name. He's a degenerate. That's not the point. The point is, relatives of the people he murdered publicly forgave him. They said it was what God would want, what Jesus would want, to forgive that misguided man for murdering people in a church. I never understood that, how anyone could *forgive* something like that."

"But now you do, is that it? You brought us here to your daughter's grave to declare your forgiveness?"

"No," I said. I hoped he could hear the smile in my voice. "I came here to watch you die."

They laughed, yucking it up. All of them save Joe.

"I know you think I'm a joke, some middle-aged English teacher who believes he can morph into Batman or whatever. I'm supposed to be intimidated by your looks, your ink, your hate. I know those red laces mean you've shed blood, hurt innocent people, maybe killed them."

"That's right," Jessie said.

"I know all about it. The fourteen on your body is about saving the white children, and the eighty-eight is a stupid Hitler reference. I know the spiderweb tat on Joe's elbow means he has a confirmed kill in the name of the cause. I also know you're all idiots. I'm being sincere, not cruel. I mean, you'd have to be complete morons to believe the white doctrine nonsense. A

Jewish cabal secretly running the government? A world-wide plan to systemically infect the white race with minority impurities? Come on, really guys?"

"Fuck you, man," Jessie said.

"Shut up," Erik told him.

"We here so you can give us a book report, Mr. Eden?" Joe asked.

"Let's play a game." I stepped to the side with a showman's gesture as if to say, *ta-da!*, and there was Penelope's grave. Sticking out of the dirt was a shovel and a shotgun.

"You want me to go for that shotgun so you can hit me with the shovel."

"No, Joe, I want you to go for the shovel so I can shoot you in the face."

He looked unsure. "You're wracked with guilt. Unable to forgive yourself. If only you'd been beside your daughter when—"

I grabbed the shovel, lifted, and drove it down into the soft earth. "Come on!" I yelled. "Come and protect her!" I lifted it again and thrusted the shovel blade into the dirt. Again. Again. *"Come on! Come now!"*

"He's lost it," Erik said.

"Lemme do it," Jessie said.

"One good hit," Joe said.

"That's all it's gonna take."

And Jessie came for me.

I lifted and stabbed the ground again. I'd already dug a decent hole before Joe and his crew arrived. Shoveling at my daughter's grave dirt and watching the dark wood-line, spying for any movement, any large shadowy thing beginning to take shape. Was it there? Was it even real?

The monster protects the princess. Monsters are always.

Create what you need.

"Come on! Come and protect her! Protect the princess!" I screamed with all I had.

Again and again, I bayonetted the ground with the shovel, but Jessie was coming straight for me in slow, deliberate steps, the weighted sock swinging at his side, *tick tick,* but now speeding up, *tickticktickticktick,* and right as he was about to hit me with my own homemade weapon—

"Fuck is that?" Leroy said. He sounded terrified. "Is that a bear?"

Jessie heard "bear" and looked off toward the woods.

I swung the shovel right at him and he turned his head back in time for the shovel blade to fill his vision. It thwacked his ugly-mustachioed face dead-on in a perfect, nose-crunching, metal-vibrating donging-clang.

Blood exploded from his face.

"Now!" I screamed.

On cue, Corbet rushed from behind the elm tree, his shovel gripped over his shoulder like an enormous baseball bat ready to swing. Erik didn't even look as Corbet hit him as I'd hit Jessie, only much harder. Shovel-against-skull was the sound of a hurtled pumpkin erupting against the street. Erik's head didn't explode in a mess of pumpkin-like pulp-brains, however—he simply dropped flat to the ground, unmoving.

He might be dead.

The monster was emerging from the woods. It could be a bear, *had* to be a bear. What else could it be? But it wasn't. No bear looked like this. Even if it were some mutated, deformed monstrosity, it still would not be *this.*

Light glowed along the monster's beetle shell.

And curved in its eyes. Its *spider* eyes.

Leroy made a sound like a man trying to scream through a mouthful of food. The creature—*monster*—was coming right for him, coming on faster in a heavy gallop of hard muscles and propulsion. Leroy didn't even try to run, maybe he was too shocked or maybe he knew there was no point trying, but then he had a pistol in hand and went toward the monster, shooting at the thing, a succession of firecracker pops that sounded as weak as they were ineffective.

If any bullets hit it, there was no way to tell.

It kept charging.

Cerberus yanked to the end of his leash, barking loud, unafraid.

"What the hell . . ." Corbet standing there staring as dumbfounded as the rest of us.

I shouldn't have been surprised, I'd seen this thing before, except seeing it now confirmed that it hadn't been a delusion. This thing, this impossible creation, *was* real.

The monster was almost at Leroy. He'd stopped firing, maybe out of bullets, and watched dumbly as the beast barreled right toward him. The ground shook. The thing went up on its hind legs at the last moment and pummeled its full weight onto Leroy. He collapsed beneath it, fat body no more solid than a rotting tree in a strong wind.

One heavy paw knocked Leroy's head aside. He was twitching, spasming, but not fighting. The opportunity for that, if possible, was long gone. Then the monster lifted its head, opening its mouth wide for its fangs and elongating beetle mandibles, and with a roaring, chittering cry of triumph, it chomped into Leroy's head.

We watched.

Except Joe.

He went for the shotgun.

I turned, bringing up the shovel, and swung but Joe jumped aside, snatched the shotgun out of the ground and turned—toward the thing eating Leroy.

Twenty feet away, Leroy made the last sound of his life, a garbled almost-scream, before his head crunched inside the monster's jaw. I thought again of an exploding pumpkin, the heavy innards-spewing splash of it. The beast lifted on its hind legs and stomped on Leroy's chest. Bones shattered and fatty guts wet the grass.

Joe stood gawking, his face a pale slate of fear.

He was Macbeth gone mad at the sight of Banquo's ghost: *Hence, horrible shadow! Unreal mock'ry hence!*

He pumped the shotgun's forestock, that distinctive, intimidating sound, an action which loads a bullet into firing position. If there'd been any bullets.

Click.

Click. Click.

"Sorry, Joe," I said. "Forgot the bullets."

I swung the shovel and hit him in the side, the blade flat like a giant's palm. Joe stumbled sideways. He aimed the shotgun at me, pumped it again, and pulled the trigger. Click. I shrugged and Corbet's shovel hit him on the other side of the chest, the blade cutting into him sideways like a sword. This time, Joe fell. The useless shotgun dropped from his hands.

We were on him immediately, our shovels pushed into the base of his neck. He grabbed the blades but had no leverage. We pressed down. He gagged and choked and squirmed. We could kill him with a little more pressure.

Jessie woke with a retching snort of blood.

I glared down at Joe. "My daughter would want me to forgive you. She believed in forgiveness and love and peace."

"But not you, that it?" Joe said, voice strained yet enraged. "You gonna kill me because you don't want peace, just revenge? Damn the consequences. You'll never make it in prison."

Cerberus was barking, rapid, frantic.

"Fuck is that?" Jessie said in a child's horrified screech.

The monster went for him, the ground earthquaking beneath its attack.

"No, Joe, I'm not going to kill you, but I will never forgive you. I will carry this hate in my heart the rest of my life, and each day I wake, that hate will be there to weigh me down, and I'll carry it with me, and I'll get good at masking it, hiding it, and only taking it out when I want. It won't control me, but I'll never let it go. Not ever."

Jessie was crying, begging for his mommy.

"I said I wanted to exterminate you, but you're not like a bug, Joe. That's insulting to insects. No, you're nothing more than a clog in a drain. Luckily, that's easily handled."

From my cargo pocket, I removed the white bottle with a large red skull and crossbones on it. DANGER - POISON - CAUSES SEVERE BURNS - CORROSIVE TO EYES AND SKIN - HARMFUL OR FATAL IF SWALLOWED.

Joe tried to be brave. I'll grant him that much. " 'So foul and fair a day,' Mr. English Teacher?"

I grinned down at him. "Fuck Shakespeare."

And poured the drain cleaner on his pretty movie-star face.

Except someone grabbed my wrist, squeezed it hard. Penelope. But it wasn't physical strength that stopped my hand. It was her stare. Her eyes were big and black, except they glowed so brightly, crammed with a galaxy of stars. She contained a whole universe inside of her.

"It's okay, Dad. I love you. Always."

The starlight collapsed to black and her eyes gleamed shiny and lifeless.

"No . . ."

I was in the street on my knees, the air a burning stink, my ears echoing a mad engine howl and the frantic screams of those who got away. My daughter was twisted unnaturally, bloody, not breathing. No, please, God, no. Her fingers twitched. They touched my hand. *Alive.* She was still alive. I cried out. Screamed for help. I don't know how. I had no breath. Only shock and pain. My chest crushed inward. Penelope's mouth opened as she tried to speak, her cheek grating against the concrete, and then she stopped. Her fingers dropped from my hand. I was alone in the street.

Joe gawked up at her. At my daughter, who was murdered by one of his idiot followers but who right now in this place at this moment was very much alive.

She leaned down toward him.

"BOO!"

Joe screamed and she was gone. Her laugh echoed.

I turned to Corbet and saw pure fear. The monster was right behind me.

Turning, I faced it.

It chuffed breath. A growling rumble in its throat. Dark phlegmy mucus slipped off its muzzle. Pieces of Leroy and Jessie dangled from its fangs. The smell was a potent earthy rot, and my reflection in all those eyes made the ground unsteady and my throat slick with bile.

We can create anything. Whatever we need.

"Go ahead." I spread my arms wide. "Do it! *Kill me!*"

It thumped closer. Its thick talons carved trenches in the earth. Closer. It snorted. Tufts of wire-stiff fur flexed along its hackles. Another few feet and it could do what I wanted it to. What I needed it to. This thing, this monster that couldn't possibly be and yet was, *it* could release me from all my pain. It stopped, opened its mouth, its jaw unhinging wider and wider, all those sharp teeth gleaming blood. It growled a high-pitched buzzing chitter.

"Kill me!"

I was bathed in blinding light.

Coming from directly overhead.

I squinted up, my eyes burning in the harsh light. I managed to block enough of it with my hands to see a shape hovering high above, its saucer-edge shiny as a polished wheel.

A flying spaceship from a science fiction film.

Or one drawn in a sketchbook.

"This means something." My voice was so small I'm not sure I even vocalized it, but I felt it, that awe, that certainty of coming up against the veil of the unknown. *Show me something, please. Show me what it all means.*

The light flickered and went out.

Stars blanketed the sky.

Joe scrambled on all-fours and launched into a sprint down the hill toward his truck, the headlights shining funnels of light.

The monster snorted a mucusy huff and went after him.

If not for the gravestones, Joe might have made it to his truck, or at least closer to it. He kept glancing back over his shoulder at the horror galloping after him and ran full-speed into a thick slab of granite. Something inside him snapped with the finality of never-to-be-healed. He crumpled onto the stone, tried to hoist himself, but it was useless. Horrified, he watched over his shoulder as the monster slowed its approach, as if relishing the moment.

He screamed a throat-destroying holler.

A coward's scream.

It didn't kill him right away. It bit him, tore flesh from his face, and stomped on his legs, and then it made a high-pitched buzzing chitter and chomped onto his torso. It dragged him backwards toward the woods. He screamed and screamed. Then he was gone into the woods wherever the monster was taking him, swallowed by the darkness.

I stared up at all those stars.

Stared.

Inside me an avalanche, a cave-in, a collapse, ribs clenching around heart and lungs, all that trapped breath, pressure pushing, nowhere to go, my teeth clamping it back, and there was the *pain*, the kind of pain you never imagine; this pain you can't ever escape because it looks at you with glazed eyes that were once your daughter's and when it speaks, its truth is yours and yours alone, living now in your veins and in your soul.

I did not want to let it go. That pain was *mine*.

It's all I had left.

But then, finally, I wept.

I screamed it all free, emptying out, and the sky opened and a heavy rain fell, a summer deluge, sudden and drenching. There was no thunder, no lightning, no clouds. Water pummeled in ferocious assault. I was soaked in seconds, but I didn't move. It rained and rained, and I cried and cried, shaking free cold tremors of hurt.

The monster came back for the others. One at a time. It fed, gnawing muscle and bone and slurping blood, and then it bit each corpse on the leg and dragged it off into the woods. The bodies left flattened wet trails in the grass.

Corbet and I watched from beneath the elm tree where we sat with our backs against the trunk. He'd gotten wet too, but I was completely soaked and shivering. But each breath I took reached deeper recesses within me. Cerberus sat next to me, surprisingly dry, and I pet him as he watched the monster and didn't even bark.

"What if that thing comes for us?"

"It won't."

He left the follow-up question unasked. Several minutes later, however, he asked if this was all a dream or a shared delusion.

"It can be whatever you want."

"That's the problem with you English teachers. Everything's up for interpretation."

"What's the scientific explanation then?"

Corbet chuckled. "Fuck if I know."

We cleaned up Penelope's gravesite, filling in the hole, adjusting the marker, and yes, I wanted her to appear once more but I knew she wouldn't.

And she didn't.

Chapter Thirty-Two

In mid-October, we held a memorial for Penelope in the cemetery. They installed her gravestone that Saturday morning. The air was crisp and refreshing and the sky was an almost too glorious light blue with painting-perfect fluffy white clouds.

A detective questioned me after Joe and his crew vanished. His truck had been abandoned at the cemetery and there were blood trails leading into the woods, but they never found bodies.

"You know anything about that?" Detective King asked.

"Not a thing. Why?"

"Looks like maybe they were there to desecrate your daughter's grave. My condolences, by the way."

"Thank you, but I don't know anything about that."

The detective eyed me a moment and adjusted his tie. "I know you bought a gun that day. You sure there's nothing you want to tell me?"

I shook my head. "What do *you* think happened to them?"

He paused for almost half a minute and his lips curved up at the corners. "No idea, and, quite frankly, I don't care."

In the cemetery, it was me and Corbet and his family and two dozen of Penelope's friends, including Cassidy, her leg healed.

Julie was there, too.

She held my hand as we encircled the grave. She hadn't had a bout of the "crazies" in a long, long time, and was back at home with me most days. She still spent a lot of time at the women-only house in town. They were good for her. They helped her. She needed my help, too, and I hadn't given her that. I apologized. This was in late summer. I went to that Victorian house and said I was sorry. "I put all my energy into Penelope," I told her. "I didn't know how to help you, so I turned away from you. Abandoned you. I should've been there for you. You're my wife, and I love you. I'm sorry."

No priest at the memorial. No ceremony. No suit, either. It was family and friends gathered together on a beautiful day.

I thought Mercedes might show but she didn't, and maybe that was a good thing. A week after Joe and his cronies found death at the claws and fangs of an impossible beast, I stopped by the shitty shotgun house where she lived. Alone.

Cerberus jumped out of the car and ran to her, tail wagging. It was fun having him at my house, but Mercedes needed him more. "Where's everybody else?"

"I don't know. I keep expecting them to come back. No one yet." She looked rested, on her way toward healthy.

"You need anything? Money?"

"No." She looked around, as if afraid someone was listening. "Joe had a stash, ten thousand, maybe more."

"Enough to start a new life," I said.

"It's like they vanished. Did you do something to them?"

"We create what we need," I said. "Now, you can create what *you* need."

I wasn't planning on giving a speech at Penelope's gravesite, but there I was, standing in a circle before my daughter's headstone and everyone hushing around me.

"What's done can't be undone. Shakespeare wrote that, and if Penelope were here, she'd roll her eyes and tell me this is a memorial, not a class lecture. She was the bravest, kindest, funniest, most wonderful person I've ever known. We were blessed to know her. She was killed by a man with hate in his heart, and I had hate in my heart for him, too. I wanted vengeance. How could my beautiful daughter die and that man and his disgusting friends keep living? I wanted them to die, and I wanted to be the one who did it."

Julie squeezed my hand. Sunlight flickered around a cloud.

I wanted to be the one who did it is what I'd told the district attorney when he called me in September. He wanted me to testify at the Tanner Wyatt trial. Logan "Rando" Repp, who'd been hit by that Dodge Charger as well, never made it out of the hospital. I'd gotten my wish. "Don't worry, Mr. Eden, the justice system will get the vengeance you want, and you don't have to get your hands dirty. We're charging Wyatt with two murders. He's never getting out of jail."

Get your hands dirty. I was staring at Penelope's grave. That night with Corbet right here in this spot, I'd gotten on my hands and knees to fill in the hole I'd dug that summoned the monster, and I smoothed the dirt flat. I was soaked and my hands were shaking. I'd grieved fierce, body-wracking tears, but it left me hollow and raw.

I'd told Joe I would carry my hate for him the rest of my life, that it would be there but that I wouldn't let it control me. The word for that is bravado. Or delusion. I fell asleep every night with hate in my heart and woke every morning with renewed rage. Joe was gone, devoured by an imaginary monster, but my child was still dead. No Lazarus moment for her. It wasn't fair. I'd screamed out my pain, grieved into a torrential downpour, but all it did was make more room for anger.

"My heart will never stop hurting," I said with Penelope's grave before me and everyone listening. "I'm angry, too. So damn angry. I believed that if I could hurt the people who hurt my daughter, I'd feel better. It doesn't work that way. The hurt is okay, it's right to feel it and good, but anger is poison. I don't want it anymore."

Julie was on one side of me and Corbet on the other. This time, *he* squeezed my hand.

A brisk wind swept through the cemetery. We were in T-shirts, pink with my daughter's face on them. It was cold, but the sun was warm.

"I want to be the man my daughter believed I could be. I don't know if I will ever forgive. How could I forgive those who hurt my daughter? How can I forgive myself as I watched it happen? I'm not there yet. But what I can do, what I *promise* to do, is find peace. We're all of us haunted by the familiar devils of hate and pain and grief and mercy and forgiveness. They challenge us to be better, they torment us when we fail, but they might also lead us where we need to go. That is the path of healing. If Penelope were here, she'd say that what matters in this world is kindness. Love. She'd say love is what we need and if we believe in it, we can create it."

I looked at all the faces looking at me. I thought Penelope might be among them. She wasn't, but she was with us. I had no doubt.

I raised my poster-board sign overhead and everyone else raised there's as well. A sea of pinks and blues and yellows, of hearts and glittery letters.

Love is life, my sign proclaimed.

I have my memories of Penelope, and I have this story. *You create what you need*. I wrote all this sitting at Penelope's desk, that quote right there anytime I needed it. Did all of this happen? Was that monster real? Does it matter? This is more than a story, this thing I've written. Such as it is, it's what *I* needed. It's healing.

It's my path toward peace.

There are empty devils everywhere. We fill them with our fears and sometimes they wreak havoc in our lives. They can hurt and they can kill, but they don't have to control us. We can choose something different. We can choose love.

On that beautiful October day, we marched out of the cemetery, down the road, and into town where we stopped traffic

while we chanted for peace and hope and cheered and clapped
and danced.

Where there's love there's life.

Always.

Quick Favor

Thank you so much for dedicating your time to reading this book! May we ask a quick favor?

Will you please take a moment to leave a review on Amazon, Goodreads, or wherever you purchased the book? Your words have power. Your review can help this book reach more readers. We appreciate you!

Author's Notes and Acknowledgments

Some ideas I know exactly their origin. August 12, 2017, white supremacists staged a Unite the Right rally in Charlottesville, Virginia, and Alex Fields Jr. drove his Dodge Challenger through a crowd of counter-protestors, injuring dozens and killing Heather Heyer. President Trump would remark that there were "fine people on both sides."

My intention was not to write a "political" book, but all books are political. All of our language is political. How we speak of anything is informed by our insight, our history, our prejudice. Are there in fact "very fine people on both sides"? A fascinating question. One demanding nuanced analysis. What does courage look like to the white supremacist? Is a father's love the same for his daughter regardless of political affiliation?

Or maybe the white supremacist Nazis can go fuck themselves.

All that isn't exactly beside the point, but it's too much in the brain and not where I enjoy writing best—deep in the heart.

What if a Charlottesville-type tragedy occurred in a small New York town? How would the parents react if it were their child who was run over? What would that do to a person? How could you even conceive of healing? Could you grant forgiveness the way many victims' families forgave Dylan Roof after he murdered nine people inside a church in Charleston in 2015?

That's how this story started—a grieving father confronting the neo-Nazis he blames for his daughter's death.

Some books take a long time. They gestate.

I wrote the first four chapters longhand in 2019?, and I set them aside until some time in 2021 or 2022, and then David Eden told me the rest of his story.

There are numerous versions of this story. There's one that includes a complete narrative arc for Julie told from her point of view, and an entire finale I never wrote in which the women from that Victorian house literally tear the white supremacists to pieces in the graveyard, my homage to the ferocious Handmaids doling out brutal justice in the night woods as Lesley Gore sings "You Don't Own Me." There's another version where David and Corbet devise an elaborate scheme to trick Joe and his cronies (and misdirect the reader in the name of a surprising and satisfying didn't-see-that-coming showdown), but alas, I didn't have the writing chops to pull that off.

This book could have been quite the mess.

All these disparate ideas I had. What I should do is take up a knife and slice away the skin and sinew, worm my fingers around the bloody heart and squeeze. But the heart is so full of empty devils, and here in my story we've got Shakespeare, white supremacists, a women's maybe-cult, a grieving father, a carrion monster born right from a character's imagination, cruelty, bravery, grief, awe, and *Close Encounters of the Third Kind*.

That's what makes the heart beat. What gets the words on the page.

Grief horror is its own powerful sub-genre, and I must give a special shoutout to Clay McLeod Chapman's masterful *Kill Your Darling*, which I read while working through development edits on this book and whose writing taunted and inspired me to discover what I might accomplish.

My wife and I don't have any children. Perhaps this is because, at least in part, I'm terrified of my own child dying. No matter the cause, I know I would suffer rage. I would rail against the universe. I would not forgive, not ever—be the culprit cancer or heart defect or accident or hate-spewing maniac behind the wheel of a speeding car.

Friends and colleagues have wondered why children-in-peril is a common theme in my work. I grew up reading Stephen King, so if your formative horror reads are *Cujo* and *Pet Sematary*, I think you can be forgiven for fixating on childhood mortality.

I've suffered plenty of deaths, too—my uncle when I was 9, my father when I was 11, my grandmother when I was 14, my aunt when I was 26, my mother when I was 35, and cats and dogs, as much my family as people (Dusty, Sandy, Silky, Sammy, Dasher, Susie, Buddy, Misty, Margot, Elsa, Indy, Logan, and even as I write this our cat Lily is telling me with her 19-year-old glazed eyes that it's time; Christ, that's some list and it's only getting longer*).

Let me be straightforward about this book: I didn't want David to learn that he needed to let go of his anger. I wanted his anger to win out. I wanted a finale in which his anger empowered him to beat the hell out of those idiot white supremacists. Burn them, dismember them, pure vengeful fury.

The writer can be god, if he or she chooses, but the writer is wiser to be an "amanuensis," which is apparently the term for someone who takes dictation. Faulkner said something about chasing behind his characters, frantically scribbling down everything that happens. That's good advice.

David wanted to let go of his hate, even if it took a supernatural creature to make him realize it. Holding onto that hate, onto that grief, it kills you. Forgiveness, though? I couldn't get there. I couldn't write the scene where he forgives the man who murdered his daughter. Is that David telling me he isn't there yet as the final words of this book put him right where his daughter died, protesting exactly as she did? Or is this a personal hangup of mine hindering David's journey? He won't forgive because I can't forgive.

One last thing: this is a horror novel.

The scariest scene for me is when Joe Klegg gives his what-it-means-to-be-an-American diatribe. It terrifies me in ways no supernatural monster ever could. What's that song in *South Pacific* about being carefully taught? Education is how we construct understanding and the arts is how we cultivate empathy. Words and story are distinctly human. Stories are empathy machines.

(Mini-rant: AI can't teach me anything about being human because it isn't a human with its own experiences and perspectives. AI is not a tool; it's a scapegoat in the name of a shortcut. It can create because it recognizes patterns, but it can't give me something with a beating heart, something I'd believe, something that would make my gut believe, as Tim O'Brien has said.)

Imagination is what I'm talking about. Without my imagination, I'm pretty sure I go crazy. So, let me thank my parents first. They raised me in a world of books and movies and unrestricted playtime. My mother let me read Stephen King, whose books seduced me and forever changed my life. And his books led me to Peter Straub's and Elmore Leonard's and on and on. (I'm trying to channel Leonard in this book's opening pages.) Special thanks to William Shakespeare for writing truth that wouldn't hit me until I was forty and ready for it. Thanks to Joe Hill for saying that everything you write is a first draft of something else. Thanks to Paul Tremblay for wearing his influences on his literary sleeves. Thanks to Stephen Graham Jones for saying you've got to write yourself dry and then really dig deep. And thanks to Stephen Spielberg for *Close Encounters*, all that grandeur and awe and possibility. Obsession, too, and the need for it all to mean something.

Immense thanks to Sobelo Books. Lucas and Les are good people and good writers. They believed in my book, and they believed I could make it even better, squeeze its bloody heart, and I thank them for pushing me to dig deeper, polish my prose so its sharp edge could cut no matter what page you open. Quick shoutout to Christine Harrold for organizing Horror Reader Weekend at Bear Mountain in November 2024, such a blast, and I got to meet Lucas in person. Let's do it again soon.

Most importantly, thank you to my wife, Jenn, who supports my writing "crazies" and who opens my heart again and again to a life freed of anger and full of love. She's never said it, but every day she proves its truth, where there's love, there's life.

Be well, be happy, be kind,

Chris DiLeo

December 1, 2024

*I wrote this in the morning, and twelve hours later we said goodbye to Lily. A vet came to our house and Lily found peace on a soft blanket on top of my *Jaws* rug not four feet from where I write this. These last several years, her favorite spot was in the heated cat bed in my office. She was with me as I wrote every word of this book. So, here in this footnote I also dedicate this book to her.

About the Author

DiLeo is the author of numerous books. He is a high school English teacher in New York's Hudson Valley, and a member of the Horror Writers Association. His work is visceral, emotional, and entertaining. He loves exploring the inner-realms of characters and then bringing on the horror. DiLeo's fondness for the unquiet coffin was fostered by an academic father whose love of the macabre brought local notoriety every Halloween when he transformed the DiLeo lawn into a haunted graveyard. In death, DiLeo's father left behind a coffin-shaped bookcase containing his favorite horror novels. Ever since DiLeo inherited that coffin, he has been enthralled by (and afraid of) the chaos lurking beneath the commonplace, the horrors of men and the supernatural.

www.ingramcontent.com/pod-product-compliance
Lightning Source LLC
Chambersburg PA
CBHW031038310726

48969CB00007B/2032